The Three Naughty Children
and other stories

Enid Blyton

The Three Naughty Children
and other stories

Illustrated by
Eileen A. Soper

ARMADA

First published in Great Britain in 1950
by Macmillan & Co. Ltd

*The Most Surprising Chair, The Boy
Who Threw Stones, The Bad Little Boy,
The Tell-Tale Bird, He Forgot His Ears,
He Didn't Think* and *The Boy Who
Put Out His Tongue*
first published as part of
A Book of Naughty Children
in 1944 by Methuen & Co. Ltd

Republished by Dragon Books 1974
This Armada edition 1989
Armada is an imprint of the Children's Division,
part of the Collins Publishing Group,
8 Grafton Street, London W1X 3LA

Printed and bound in Great Britain, by
William Collins Sons & Co. Ltd, Glasgow

CONTENTS

THE THREE NAUGHTY
CHILDREN

One day Queen Peronel's cook heard a knocking at her kitchen door. She opened it and saw a ragged pedlar there, his tray of goods in front of him.

'Can I sell you something?' said the pedlar. 'Red ribbons, silver thimbles, honey-chocolate, high-heeled shoes – I have them all here.'

'Nothing today, thank you,' said the cook. But the pedlar would not go.

'I am tired with walking many miles,' he said. 'Let me come in and rest a little. See, I will wipe my feet well on the mat so that I shall not dirty your clean kitchen floor.'

So the cook let him come in and sit down on her oldest chair for a little while. But when he had gone she missed three things, and flew to tell Queen Peronel.

'Oh, Your Highness!' she cried, bursting into the drawing-room where the Queen sat knitting a jersey. 'Oh, Your Highness, a pedlar has stolen your blue milk-jug, your little silver spoon and your wooden porridge plate! Oh, whatever shall I do!'

Now these three things were all full of magic and the Queen treasured them very much. The blue milk-jug had the power of pouring out perfectly fresh milk twice a day, which was very useful for the Queen's nurse, for she had two little princesses and a prince to look after in the royal nursery. The silver spoon would make anyone hungry if he put it into his mouth, and this, too, was *very* useful if any of the royal children wouldn't eat a meal.

The wooden porridge plate could play a tune all the time that porridge was eaten from it, so the children loved it very much. Queen Peronel was dreadfully upset when she heard that all these things had been stolen.

'What was the pedlar like?' she asked. 'I will have him captured and put into prison.'

But alas, when the cook told her about the pedlar's looks, the Queen knew that he was no pedlar but a wizard who had dressed himself up to steal her treasures. She called the King and he really didn't know what to do.

'That wizard is too powerful for us to send to prison,' he said, shaking his head. 'He won't give us back those three things if we ask him nicely, for he will say he didn't steal them. I really do *not* know what to do.'

Now when the two little princesses and the prince heard how the wizard had stolen their milk-jug, porridge plate and spoon, they were very angry.

'Send a hundred soldiers to him, Father, and capture him!' cried Roland, the little prince, standing straight and tall in front of the King.

'Don't be silly, my dear child,' said the King. 'He would turn them all into wolves and send them howling back here. You wouldn't like that, would you?'

'Well, Father, send someone to steal all the things from *him*,' said Rosalind, the eldest child, throwing back her golden curls.

'You don't know what you are talking about,' said the King crossly. 'Go back to the nursery, all of you, and play at trains.'

They went back to the nursery, but they didn't play at trains. They sat in a corner and talked. Rosalind and Roland were very fierce about the stealing of their magic things. Then Roland suddenly thought of an idea.

'I say, Rosalind, what about dressing up as a wizard myself and going to call on the wizard who took away our things? Perhaps I could make him give them back. *I'm* not afraid of any old wizard!'

'I shall come, too,' said Rosalind, who liked to be in everything.

'And so shall I,' said Goldilocks, the youngest of them all.

'You're too little,' said Roland.

'I'm *not!*' said Goldilocks. 'I shall cry if you don't let me come.'

'All right, all right, you can come,' said Roland, 'but if you get turned into a worm or something, don't blame *me!*'

Then they made their plans, and very queer plans they were, too. They were all to slip out of bed that night and go downstairs, dressed, when nobody was about. Roland was to get his father's grandest cloak and feathered hat, and the two girls were to take with them a pair of bellows each, a box of fireworks from the firework cupboard, and two watering-cans full of water. How strange!

They were most excited. They could hardly wait until the clock struck eleven and everyone else was in bed. Then they dressed and went downstairs. Soon Roland was wrapped in his

father's wonderful gold and silver cloak, with big diamonds at the neck and round the hem. On his curly head he put his father's magnificent feathered hat, stuffed with a piece of paper inside to make it fit. Then, with their burden of bellows, fireworks and watering-cans, they set off to the wizard's little house on the hillside not far off.

It was all in darkness save for one light in the nearest window.

'He's still up,' said Roland. 'Good! Now, you two girls, you know what to do, don't you? As soon as you hear me shouting up the chimney, do your part. And if you make a mistake, Goldilocks, I'll pull your hair tomorrow, so there!'

'Help me to get the ladder out of the garden shed,' said Rosalind as they came near to the cottage. Roland and the two girls silently carried the ladder to the cottage and placed it softly

against the roof. Then up went the two princesses, as quietly as cats. In half a minute they were sitting beside the chimney, their bellows, fireworks and watering-cans beside them.

It was time for Roland to do his part. He wrapped the big cloak around his shoulder and strode up to the door. He hammered on it with a stone he had picked up and made a tremendous noise. The wizard inside nearly jumped out of his skin.

'Now who can this be?' he wondered, getting up. 'Some great witch or enchanter, hammering like that on my door!'

He opened the door and Roland strode in, not a bit nervous.

'Good evening, wizard,' he said. 'I am Rilloby-Rimmony-Ru, the Enchanter from the moon. I have heard that you can do wondrous things. Show me some.'

The wizard looked at Roland's grand cloak and hat and thought he must indeed be a rich and great enchanter. He bowed low.

'I can command gold to come from the air, silver to come from the streams, and music from the stars,' he said.

'Pooh!' said Roland rudely, 'anyone can do that! Can you call the wind and make it do your bidding?'

'Great sir, no one can do that,' answered the wizard, mockingly.

'Ho, you mock at me, do you?' said Roland. He went to the chimney and shouted up it. 'Wind, come down to me and show this poor wizard how you obey my commands!'

At once Rosalind and Goldilocks began to work the bellows down the chimney, blowing great puffs of air down as they opened and shut the bellows. The smoke from the fire was blown all over the room and the wizard began to cough. He looked frightened.

'Enough, enough!' he cried. 'You will smoke me out. Command the wind to stop blowing down my chimney.'

'Stop blowing, wind!' commanded Roland, shouting up the chimney. At once the two girls on the roof stopped working the bellows, and the smoke went up the chimney in the ordinary way.

'Wonderful, wonderful!' said the wizard, staring at Roland in amazement. 'I have never seen

anyone make the wind his servant before.'

'That's nothing,' said Roland, grandly. 'I can command the rain, too.'

'Bid it come, then,' said the wizard, trembling. Roland shouted up the chimney. 'Rain, come at my bidding!' At once Rosalind and Goldilocks poured water down the chimney from their watering-cans and it hissed on the fire and spat on the hearth. The wizard leapt back in alarm.

'Stop the rain!' he cried. 'It will put out my fire if it rushes down my chimney like that.'

Roland, who didn't at all want the fire to be put out, hastily shouted to the rain to stop, and the two little girls put their watering-cans down, giggling to hear the astonished cries of the wizard.

'Surely you can do no greater thing than these!' said the wizard to Roland.

'Well, I can command the thunder and lightning, too,' said Roland. 'Wait. I will call down some for you to see.'

Before the frightened wizard could stop him Roland shouted up the chimney again. 'Thunder and lightning, come down here!'

Rosalind dropped a handful of fireworks down at once. They fell into the flames and exploded with an enormous bang, flashing brightly. The wizard yelled in alarm and ran into a corner. Rosalind dropped down some more fireworks, and two squibs hopped right out of the fire to the corner where the wizard was hiding.

'Oh, oh, the thunderstorm is coming after me!' he shouted. 'Take it away, great Enchanter, take it away!'

Roland badly wanted to laugh, but he dared not even smile. Another batch of fireworks fell down the chimney, and the wizard rushed away again and fell over a stool.

'Stop, thunder and lightning!' called Roland up the chimney. At once the girls stopped throwing down fireworks and there was peace and quiet in the room, save for the wizard's moans of fright.

'Am I not a powerful enchanter?' asked Roland, grandly. 'Would you not like to know my secrets?'

'Oh, Master, would you tell me them?' cried the wizard, delighted.

'I will write them down on a piece of paper for you,' said Roland, 'but you must not look at it until tomorrow morning. And now, what will you give me in return?'

'Sacks of gold, cart-loads of silver,' cried the wizard.

'Pooh!' said Roland, scornfully. 'What's the use of those to me? I am richer than everyone in the world put together.'

'Then look round my humble dwelling and choose what takes your fancy,' said the wizard at once. 'See, I have strange things here – what would you like?'

Roland glanced round quickly and saw the

blue milk-jug, the silver spoon and the porridge plate on a shelf.

'Hm!' he said, 'I don't see much that I like. Wait! Here is a pretty jug. I will take that in return for the secret of the wind. And here is a dainty silver spoon. That shall be my reward for the secret of the rain. Then what shall I take

for the secret of the thunder and lightning? Ah, here is a porridge plate I shall love to use. Wizard, I will take all these. Now see – here is an envelope. Inside you will find written the secret of the wind, the rain and the thunderstorm you have seen here tonight. Do not open it until tomorrow morning.'

He took the jug, the spoon and the porridge dish, and strode out of the door, the wizard bowing respectfully in front of him. Rosalind and Goldilocks had already climbed down the ladder and were waiting for him. They ran as fast as they could with all their watering-cans, bellows and other things, laughing till they cried when they thought of the clever tricks they had played.

And when the King and Queen heard of their prank they didn't know whether to scold or praise.

'You naughty, brave, rascally, daring scamps!' cried the Queen. 'Why, you might have been turned into frogs!'

As for the wizard, when he opened the envelope the next morning and saw what was written there, he was very puzzled indeed. For this is what Roland had written: 'The secret of the wind is Bellows. The secret of the rain is Watering-cans. The secret of the thunderstorm is Fireworks. Ha! ha!'

And now the poor wizard is wandering all over the world trying to find someone wise and clever enough to tell him the meaning of the Bellows, the Watering-cans and the Fireworks, but nobody likes to!

THE TWO GOOD FAIRIES

David and Ruth lived in Primrose Cottage, and next door to them was Daffodil Cottage. An old man lived there, very fond of his garden, which was just a little piece like theirs.

One day the old man fell ill and had to go away to be nursed. David and Ruth peeped over the fence at his garden, which was full of daffodils and primroses.

'Old Mr Reed will be sorry to leave his lovely daffodils before they are over,' said Ruth. 'I wonder if his servant will look after his garden for him.'

'Mr Reed was a cross old man,' said David. 'He used to frown if we shouted or made a noise.'

'And he hated to let us get a ball if it went over the fence,' said Ruth.

'He was never well,' said their mother. 'That is why he was cross. I expect if he had been well and strong like you he would have been jolly and good-tempered.'

The cottage next door was shut up and the hard-working little servant went back to her mother. There was no one to look after the garden, and as soon as the daffodils and primroses were over, the garden beds became full of weeds. The little lawn grew long and untidy, and thistles grew at the end of the garden.

'Isn't it a pity?' said Ruth, looking over the fence at the untidy garden. 'It used to be so nice in the summer-time, full of flowers. Now it is like a field!'

'I wonder when old Mr Reed will come back,' said David.

'Mother says he is coming back in June,' said Ruth. 'Our garden will look lovely then, but his will be dreadful.'

'Let's go and buy our seeds tomorrow,' said David. 'We ought to be planting them now, you know, else our gardens will be late with their summer flowers.'

They emptied out their money-box and counted their money. They had plenty to buy seeds.

'I wish we had enough to buy a nice wheelbarrow, a new watering-can and a spade,' said David longingly. 'All our garden things are getting old. Shall we ask Mother if she'll buy us some new ones?'

But Mother said no. 'I can't afford it,' she said. 'I am saving up to buy a new hoover, because mine is falling to bits. I'll see about your garden tools after I've bought a new hoover.'

'Oh dear,' said Ruth, 'that won't be for ages!'

The two children went off to the seedsman to buy their garden seeds. They bought candytuft, poppies, nasturtiums, virginia stock, love-in-a-mist and cornflowers – all the things that most children love to grow in their gardens. Then back they went to plant them.

They were very good little gardeners. They knew just how to get the beds ready, and how to shake the seed gently out of the packets so that not too much went into one place. They watered their seeds carefully and kept the weeds from the beds. Mother was quite proud of the way they kept their little gardens.

As they were planting their seeds Ruth had a good idea. She sat back on the grass and told it to David.

'I say, David, we've plenty of seeds this year, haven't we?' she said. 'Well, let's go and plant some next door in the little round bed just in front of the window where the old man sits every day. Even if his garden is in a dreadful state he will be able to see one nice flowery bed! It would be such a nice surprise for him!'

David thought it was a good idea. So when they had finished planting their seeds in their own little gardens the two children ran into the garden next door. Then they began to work very hard indeed.

The round bed was covered with weeds! So before any seeds were planted all the dandelions, buttercups and other weeds had to be dug

up and taken away. Then the bed was dug well over by David, and Ruth made the earth nice and fine.

Then they planted the seeds. In the middle they put cornflowers because they were nice and tall. Round them they put candytuft, with poppies here and there. In front they put love-in-a-mist with nasturtiums in between, and to edge the bed they planted seeds of the gay little virginia stock. They were so pleased when they had finished, for the bed looked very neat and tidy.

'There! That's finished,' said David. 'Now we've only got to come in and weed and water, and the bed will look lovely in the summertime! How surprised old Mr Reed will be!'

You should have seen how those seeds grew. It was wonderful. The children's gardens looked pretty enough, but the round bed next door was marvellous.

The cornflowers were the deepest of blues, and the candytuft was strong and sturdy. The virginia stock was full of buds.

'Old Mr Reed is coming back tomorrow,' Ruth in excitement. 'Won't he be surprised!'

He did come back – and he *was* surprised! The children peeped over the fence and saw him looking out of his window in the very greatest astonishment. He saw them and waved to them.

'Hallo, Ruth and David,' he said. 'Just look

at that round bed! Isn't it a picture? I was so sad when I came back thinking that I wouldn't have any flowers in my garden this summer – and the first thing I saw was this lovely bed full of colour. Do *you* know who planted the seeds?'

David and Ruth didn't like to say that they had done it.

'Perhaps it was the fairies,' said Mr Reed. 'I shouldn't be a bit surprised, would you? Well, I shall have to reward them for such a kind deed. I wonder whether one of you would come over tonight after the sun has gone down and water the bed for me? I don't expect the fairies will come now I'm back, do you?'

That evening the children took their old leaky watering-can next door and went to water the round bed. Mr Reed watched them from the window. Ruth and David saw something by the bed – and what do you think it was?

There was a fine new wheelbarrow, and inside

it were two strong spades and a perfectly splendid new red watering-can. There was a note inside the barrow too, that said: 'A present for the kind fairies who gave me such a nice surprise.'

The children didn't know *what* to do. Did Mr Reed really think it was the fairies that had worked so hard? Oh, what lovely garden tools these were – just what they needed so badly. They stood and looked at them.

'How do you like your new tools?' shouted Mr Reed from his window.

'Oh, are they for *us*?' cried the children in delight. 'It says in the note that they are for the good fairies.'

'Well, didn't you act like good fairies?' said the old man, smiling. 'You gave me a wonderful surprise, and now I'm giving you one. You did a very kind deed to a cross, bad-tempered old man. But I'm better now, and so is my temper, especially since I've had such a lovely surprise. So I hope you will often come to tea with me and play with the new puppy I have bought. Now water my garden and then take your things home to show your mother.'

'Oh, thank you *so* much,' said the children, so excited that they could hardly hold the watering-can properly. Whatever would Mother say when she heard what had happened?

Mother was delighted.

'You deserve your surprise,' she said. 'You

were kind to someone you didn't very much like, and now you have made a friend and had a lovely present.'

You should see David and Ruth gardening now with all their new tools. They are as happy as can be – and all because Ruth had a good idea and was kind to a cross old man.

THE NEWSPAPER DOG

Once upon a time there was a little dog called Tips. He belonged to Mrs Brown who lived in Primrose Cottage at the end of Cherry Village.

He was a useful little dog. He guarded the house each night for Mrs Brown. He kept her company when she was alone. He barked at any tramp who came up the front path – and once each week he fetched a newspaper for her from old Mr Jonathan who lived all by himself in a little house on the hillside.

Mr Jonathan bought the newspaper himself, and read it. Then he lent it to Mrs Jones, and after that she passed it on to someone else. She couldn't often find time to go to fetch the paper herself, so Tips fetched it for her.

He started off each Thursday evening, ran all the way down the village street, went over the bridge that crossed the stream and up the hillside to Mr Jonathan's cottage. He jumped up at the door and pushed it open. Then in he would trot and look for Mr Jonathan.

The old man always had the paper ready for him, neatly folded up with a piece of string round it. He put the packet into Tips' mouth and off the little dog would go, running all the way home again, not stopping for anything until he reached Primrose Cottage and could drop the paper at Mrs Jones's feet.

One day Mr Jonathan thought he would do some spring-cleaning. So he called on Mrs Jones and asked her to lend him her ladder.

'Dear me, what do you want to go climbing about on ladders for?' asked Mrs Jones in surprise. 'You'll fall off, Mr Jonathan, and hurt yourself.'

'Indeed I shan't!' said the old man. 'I'm going to paint my ceiling white, Mrs Jones. It is very dirty. So lend me your step-ladder, there's a good soul.'

'It's in the shed,' said Mrs Jones. 'You can have it if you want it. But do pray be careful, Mr Jonathan, for it's not a very steady pair of steps.'

Mr Jonathan found the ladder and took it home. He mixed some whitening and started to do his ceiling. It looked lovely! All day he worked at it, and then went to bed.

He began again next day, whistling to himself, sloshing about on the ceiling with the

28

whitewash, quite enjoying himself. And then a dreadful thing happened.

The postman dropped some letters in the letterbox and gave such a loud rat-a-tat that the shock made old Mr Jonathan fall off his ladder. Down he went – and when he tried to get up he found that he couldn't.

'Oh dear, oh dear, I must have sprained my ankle, or broken my leg, or something,' the old man groaned. 'Whatever shall I do? Nobody else will come today, and I can't send anyone for the doctor. I have no neighbours to call to. I am all alone!'

He lay there on the floor, groaning. He really didn't know what he was going to do. Perhaps he would have to stay there all night long. If only somebody would come! But there was nobody to come at all.

And then, just as he was thinking that, Mr

Jonathan heard the sound of pitter-pattering feet, and someone came running up the front path. Then a little body hurled itself against the door which opened at once. It was Tips, the little newspaper dog, come to get his mistress's paper, for it was Thursday evening!

He saw Mr Jonathan lying on the floor, and he was puzzled. He ran up to him and licked his hand. Then he sat down with his head on one side and said 'Woof!'

That was his way of saying: 'What's the matter? Can I help you?'

'I wish you could, Tips,' said Mr Jonathan. And then he suddenly looked more cheerful. Perhaps Tips *could* help him. He looked round. The newspaper was on a chair, already tied up with string for Mrs Jones.

'There's the paper, Tips,' said Mr Jonathan, pointing. 'Fetch it here!'

Tips saw the paper, and took it into his mouth. He was just going to run off with it when Mr Jonathan called him back.

'Don't go yet, Tips,' he said. 'Bring the paper here.'

The clever little dog understood. He ran over to Mr Jonathan with the paper in his mouth. Mr Jonathan took a pencil from his pocket and wrote in large letters across the top of the paper:

'Mrs Jones. I have fallen off the ladder. Please fetch the doctor. Mr Jonathan.'

Then he pushed the paper once more into Tips' mouth and patted the waiting dog. 'Go home now,' he said.

Tips ran off, puzzling his little head to know why Mr Jonathan was on the floor. He ran to his mistress as soon as he reached Primrose Cottage and dropped the paper at her feet. She picked it up, and caught sight of the message scribbled on the top.

'Good gracious me!' she cried. 'Poor old Mr Jonathan! He's tumbled off the ladder!'

She ran for the doctor at once, and he took her along to Mr Jonathan's in his car. It wasn't long before they had him safely in bed, his leg bandaged up, and a nice hot drink beside him.

'It was my clever little dog Tips who found Mr Jonathan when he came for my weekly paper this evening,' said Mrs Jones proudly to the doctor. 'Mr Jonathan wrote a message on the paper, and, of course, I saw it when Tips dropped the paper at my feet.'

Mr Jonathan soon got well, and one morning Mrs Jones and Tips met him going shopping for the first time, leaning on a stick.

'Now wherever are you going?' cried Mrs Jones. 'I'm sure there's no shopping so important that I can't do it for you. Whatever is it you must buy, Mr Jonathan?'

'It's something very special,' said Mr Jonathan with a smile, and he went into a little shop nearby beckoning Tips and Mrs Jones in too. And what do you suppose the special bit of shopping was? Why, a fine red collar for Tips!

'That's to show everyone what a clever, helpful little chap he is,' said Mr Jonathan, putting it round the little dog's neck. 'He really does deserve it.'

I think so, too, don't you?

MR CANDLE'S COCONUT

Mr Candle was very proud of himself. He had been to the Fair in Oak-Tree Village, and had won a coconut at the coconut shy. He had paid a penny to the man there, who had given him four balls to throw at the coconuts.

The first ball didn't go near any coconuts at all. It was a very bad shot. The second ball nearly touched the nut in the middle. The third ball went wrong somehow, and knocked off the hat of a man quite a long way away. After Mr Candle had said he was really very, very sorry, he took up his fourth and last ball, and threw that.

And, dear me, nobody was more surprised than he was to see it hit the very largest coconut of all and send it rolling to the ground! Mr Candle was simply delighted. He picked it up and took it home with him. All the way home he was making a fine plan.

He would give a Coconut Party. That would be a most unusual party. He would give his guests cocoa to drink, because that *sounded* as if it ought to go with coconut to eat. He would have a big coconut cake, some coconut ice candy and he would cut up the piece of coconut left and hand round the bits for his guests to nibble. Yes, it would be a very fine Coconut Party indeed.

So Mr Candle sent out his invitations. One went to Squiddle the Pixie. One went to Mrs Popoff the Balloon Woman, and the third one went to Mr Crinkle who painted wonderful pictures on the pavement outside the post office.

Mr Candle made his coconut cake. It was a beautiful one with coconut in it and grated coconut sprinkled on top. Then he made the coconut

34

ice candy – some in pink and some in white. It tasted lovely because Mr Candle had a bit to see.

There was just over half the coconut left when Mr Candle had finished. So he cut this up very neatly into nice little squares, and put them on a plate on the wide window-ledge ready for when his guests came that afternoon.

When they came Mr Candle was ready to greet them, dressed up in his best green and red suit, with his new pointed shoes.

'Welcome to the Coconut Party!' he said. 'I am so pleased to see you. The party is because I won a coconut at the Fair.'

'How clever of you!' said Squiddle the Pixie.

'You *must* be a good shot!' said Mr Crinkle.

'Splendid, Mr Candle!' said Mrs Popoff, beaming all over her kind red face.

Mr Candle was so pleased. He thought what nice people his friends were. Down they sat to the coconut cake, the mugs of hot, sweet cocoa, and the coconut ice laid out on a blue dish. The pieces of coconut on the window-ledge were to be eaten after tea, when they were all playing games. It would be nice to have something to nibble at then, Mr Candle thought.

They finished all the coconut cake because it was so good, and they ate all the coconut ice candy too. They drank every drop of their sweet cocoa, and then they wanted to play games.

'Let's play Hunt-the-Thimble!' said Mrs Popoff, who simply loved that game. 'Mr

Crinkle, you hide the thimble – here it is – and we'll all go out of the room while you do it.'

Out they went and shut the door. Mr Crinkle was a long time hiding the thimble. He simply could *not* think of a good place. But at last he put in on the head of a little china monkey on the mantelpiece. It looked just like a hat, and Mr Crinkle felt sure nobody would notice it was a thimble.

He called the others in, and they began to hunt. Mr. Candle saw the thimble first and he sat down at once to show the others that he had seen it. He thought it would be a good idea to offer his friends a piece of the cut-up coconut on the window-ledge as soon as they had found the thimble too.

He got up to get the plate – and my goodness me, whatever do you think? There were hardly any pieces left! Somebody had taken them!

Who could it be? It must be Mr Crinkle. He had been a long, long time hiding the thimble when all the others were outside the door. Mr Candle was cross and upset.

'Did you eat my pieces of coconut?' he suddenly said to Mr Crinkle. 'There's hardly any left. You must have eaten them when you were supposed to be hiding the thimble.'

Mr Crinkle went very red.

'No, I didn't, Mr Candle,' he said, in a very hurt voice. 'I don't eat other people's bits of coconut unless they offer them to me. I hope I

know my manners. I shan't stay and play with you any more. I shall go home.'

He put on his little red hat and walked out of the door. The others watched him go. Mr Candle felt very worried.

'He *must* have eaten the pieces of coconut,' said Squiddle the Pixie. 'He was the only one alone in the room.'

Suddenly there was a little noise at the window. Squiddle, Mr Candle and Mrs Popoff all turned round quickly. And what do you think they saw? I'll give you three guesses!

They saw three little birds there, blue-tits, dressed in pretty blue and yellow feathers – and they all picked up a piece of the white coconut and flew off out of the window in delight; for tits, as you know, love nuts, especially coconuts. I expect you have often hung up a coconut for them and watched them swinging upside down on it, pecking away as hard as they can.

'It's the tits!' cried Mr Candle. 'Look! The naughty little birds! They've taken away three more bits! They must have taken the other pieces too, but I expect Mr Crinkle was so busy trying to think of a good place to hide the thimble that he didn't notice the naughty little robbers.'

'I haven't found the thimble *yet*,' said Mrs Popoff, looking all round.

'How dreadful to tell Crinkle he had eaten the coconut when he hadn't!' said Squiddle the Pixie, looking worried. 'He was really very hurt about it.'

'I'll call him back and say I'm sorry,' said Mr Candle, shutting the window so that the blue-tits couldn't come in again. He ran to the door and looked up the street.

'Hi, Crinkle!' he shouted. 'Crinkle! Come back! You didn't eat the coconut – and we know who did.'

Mr Crinkle walked back, still looking rather cross and upset.

'It was the blue-tits who ate that coconut,' explained Mr Candle, taking his friend by the arm. 'Do forgive us for being horrid, Crinkle. There's just one piece left and you shall have that.'

Mr Crinkle was a very good-natured little fellow, and he at once forgave Mr Candle and the others for saying he had done something he hadn't. He ate the last piece of coconut and then said: 'What about a game of Blind Man's Buff?'

So they all played at Blind Man and had a lovely time together. And when they said good-bye Mr Crinkle said: 'I think a story ought to be written about how the blue-tits came and stole your coconut pieces, Mr Candle. Then it would warn people not to leave them near the window, if the blue-tits are about. Don't you think so?'

Mr Candle *did* think so – and that is why he told me to write this story!

CHIPPERDEE'S SCENT

Once upon a time the Queen of Fairyland emptied her big scent-bottle, and asked the King for some new scent.

'I don't want any I've ever had before,' she said. 'Get me something strange and lovely, something quite different from anything I've ever had.'

So the King sent out his messengers all over the place – to the topmost clouds and to the lowest caves, begging anyone who knew of a strange and lovely scent to bring it to the Queen. For reward he would give a palace set on a sunny hill, and twelve hard-working pixies to keep it beautiful.

Palaces were hard to get in those days, so anyone who had a lovely scent in bottle or jar journeyed to the Queen with it. But she didn't like any of them. She was really very hard to please.

Now there lived in a cave at the foot of a mountain a clever little pixie called Chipperdee. He spent all his days in making sweet perfumes, and he made them from the strangest things. And just about this time he finished making the strangest and loveliest perfume he had ever thought of.

He had taken twenty drops of clearest dew and imprisoned in them a beam of sunlight and a little starlight. He had taken the smell of the earth after rain and by his magic he had squeezed that into the bottle too. Then he had climbed up a rainbow and cut out a big piece of it. He heated this over a candle-flame and when it melted he let it drop into this bottle.

Then he asked a two-year-old baby to breathe her sweet breath into the full bottle – and lo and behold, the perfume was made! It smelt glorious – deep, delicious, and so sweet that whoever smelt it had to close his eyes for joy.

Now although he lived in a cave, the smell of this new perfume rose through the air and everyone who lived near smelt it. An old wizard sniffed it and thought: 'Aha! That is the scent that would please the queen mightily! I will go and seek it.'

So off he went and soon arrived at the cave where Chipperdee sat working.

'Let me buy some of that new perfume of yours to take to the Queen,' said the wizard.

'No,' said Chipperdee. 'I am going to take it myself. I shall get a palace for it and twelve hard-working servants.'

'What do you want with a palace?' asked the wizard. 'Why not let me give you a sack of gold for that bottle of scent? The Queen may not like it at all – and you will still have the sack of gold! I will not ask for it back.'

'You know perfectly well that the Queen will love this new perfume,' said Chipperdee. 'Go away, wizard. I don't like you, and you won't get any scent from me! I start tomorrow to journey to the Queen.'

The wizard scowled all over his ugly face and went away. But he made up his mind to follow Chipperdee and steal the scent from him if he could. So when he saw the pixie starting off, he made himself invisible and followed him closely all day long.

Chipperdee felt quite sure that he was being followed. He kept looking round but he could see no one at all. But he could hear someone breathing! It was very strange.

'It must be that wizard,' he thought to himself. 'He's made himself invisible. He's going to steal my bottle of scent when I sleep under a hedge tonight. Ho ho! *I'll* teach him to steal it!'

When it was dark the pixie found a nice sheltered dell. He felt all around until he found some little flowers with their heads almost hidden under heart-shaped leaves. He took out his bottle in the darkness, and emptied a little of the scent into each flower, whispering to them to hold it safely for him.

Then he filled the bottle with dew and set it beside him, curling up to go to sleep beneath a bush. He pretended to snore loudly, and almost at once he heard a rustling noise beside him, and felt a hand searching about his clothes.

The hand found the bottle and then Chipperdee heard quick footsteps going away. He sat

43

up and grinned. Ho ho! The wizard thought he
had got a fine bottle of scent – but all he had
was a bottle of plain dew!

The pixie lay down again and slept soundly.
In the morning he woke up, and looked round
at the little flowers near him. They were small
purple flowers so shy that they hid their heads
beneath their leaves. The pixie jumped up and
picked a bunch. He smelt them. Ah! His scent
was in the flowers now, and it was really wonderful.

Off he went to the court, and there he saw
the wizard just presenting the Queen with the
bottle of plain dew that he had stolen from the
pixie. How Chipperdee laughed when the
Queen threw it to the ground and scolded the
wizard for playing what she thought was a
stupid trick on her!

The pixie stepped forward and told the Queen

how the wizard had followed him and tried to steal his rare perfume. 'But, Your Majesty,' he said, 'I poured the scent into these little purple flowers, and if you will smell them, you will know whether or not you like the scent I have made.'

The Queen smelt the flowers – and when she sniffed up that deep, sweet, delicious scent she closed her eyes in joy.

'Yes!' she cried. 'I will have this scent for mine! Can you make me some, Chipperdee? Oh, you shall certainly have a palace set on a sunny hill and twelve hard-working servants to keep it for you! This is the loveliest perfume I have ever known.'

Chipperdee danced all the way back to his cave and there he made six bottles of the strange and lovely scent for the Queen. The King built him his palace on a sunny hill, and he went to live there with a little wife, and twelve hard-working servants to keep everything clean and shining.

But that isn't quite the end of the story – no, there is a little more to tell. *We* can smell Chipperdee's scent in the early springtime, for the little purple flowers he emptied his bottle into still smell of his rare and lovely perfume. Do you know what they are? Guess! Yes – violets! That's why they smell so beautiful – because Chipperdee once upon a time emptied the Queen's scent into their little purple hearts!

THE QUARRELSOME TIN SOLDIERS

Once upon a time there lived on a low wooden shelf two boxes of soldiers. One army was dressed in green and the other in red. The green army had horses to ride on, brown, black and white, but the red army had none. They carried guns, and the green horse-soldiers carried swords.

All the soldiers belonged to Kenneth. He liked them very much and often took them out to play games with him. He had a fine wooden fort, and he loved making his toy soldiers march up and down the drawbridge, and stand looking over the parapet of the fort.

The soldiers were very quarrelsome. The green horsemen hated the red foot-soldiers, and the red soldiers jeered at the green ones.

'You've only got stupid little swords,' said

46

the captain of the red army to the green captain. 'We have fine guns. *You* wouldn't be much use against an enemy!'

'Ho, wouldn't we, then!' cried the green captain in a temper. 'Well, let me tell you this – *we* ride horses. *You* have to walk everywhere.'

'We don't mind that,' said the red captain, stoutly. 'We like marching. Anyway, it's silly to have horses you can't get off. You're stuck on to your horses, and even if you wanted to march you couldn't!'

Every night the two armies quarrelled and one night there was a battle. The teddy-bear and the rabbit did their best to stop the fight, but it wasn't a bit of good.

'You'll only end in being broken to bits,' said the rabbit. 'Then what will be the use of you? Kenneth won't want to play with you any more.'

'Hold your tongue, you stupid rabbit!' said the green captain, galloping over the rabbit's toes and making him yell. 'Now, men, follow me! We'll go to the toy fort and we won't let the red soldiers in. We'll keep them out and show them what poor fellows they are.'

All the horsemen followed their captain, and the green army galloped over the floor to the gay wooden fort. It was painted red and yellow and had four wooden towers and a drawbridge. Over the bridge galloped the soldiers and, as soon as they were in, one of them pulled up the drawbridge by its little chain. Now no one else could get into the fort, except by climbing the walls.

The red soldiers had no horses so they could not go as fast as the green army. But they made haste and marched at top speed across the floor to the fort. By the time they reached it the green horse-soldiers were all in their places, looking over the top of the parapet, or cantering up and down the yard in the middle of the fort, shouting orders and feeling very important.

The red captain lined his men up in a row in front of the fort and told them to fire. Pop! Pop! Pop! The little guns went off and tiny bullets like seeds flew over the walls of the fort. Some of the green soldiers were hit and little holes were made in their tin uniforms.

They were very much upset. They shouted with rage, and galloped about, making quite a noise on the wooden floor of the fort. Then suddenly the green captain ordered the draw-bridge to be let down and commanded six of his men to ride out and make a surprise attack on the enemy soldiers outside.

The red soldiers were so astonished that some of them were ridden down before they knew what was happening. One of them had an arm broken off and another one had his leg twisted the wrong way round. A third one lost his fine helmet, and cried bitterly because he couldn't find it.

'Courage, my men!' said the captain of the

red soldiers when the green men had ridden back to the fort again. 'I am going to get the little cannon out of the nursery toy cupboard. With that we can shell down the walls of the fort, and rush in to attack the enemy.'

But the toy cannon was too heavy for the little tin soldiers to drag along. It shot peas, so it could have knocked over a great many of the green soldiers in the fort.

'Well, never mind if it's too heavy,' said the red captain. 'Look, we'll use a battering-ram instead. Here's one that will do.'

The battering-ram was really a big hoop-stick of Kenneth's. Seven soldiers picked it up and carried it to the fort. Then twelve red soldiers took hold of it, six on each side, and waited for their captain's word.

'Charge!' he cried, and fired off his little gun, making the rabbit nearly jump out of his skin, for he and the bear were almost asleep.

'Just look at those soldiers!' said the rabbit, sitting up. 'The reds are breaking down one of the walls of the fort. Wouldn't Kenneth be cross if he knew!'

'Don't you think we ought to wake him?' said the bear anxiously. 'I think he would be very sorry if the tin soldiers killed one another. He would never be able to play with them again.'

'Let's go and wake him,' said the rabbit. So without telling the soldiers the two stole out of the day nursery into the night nursery, where Kenneth slept.

Bang! Bang! Bang! The hoop-stick battering-

ram crashed against the wooden wall of the fort, and inside the green soldiers galloped about in a panic. What would they do if the wall gave way?

It did! It suddenly came away from the nails that held it and fell right down in the fort, knocking over two of the green soldiers as it fell. Then in poured the red soldiers, shouting in victory, shooting with their guns as they came.

The green soldiers soon pulled themselves together and they galloped at the enemy, slashing about with their swords, and that was how Kenneth found them when he came into the nursery with Rabbit and Teddy. He stood and

stared in astonishment at his toy soldiers fighting one another so fiercely, slashing and shooting and yelling.

'How dare you behave like this!' he said suddenly. 'You will end in being broken to bits, and I didn't buy you to fight one another. I bought you to play with! Go back to your boxes and tomorrow I will come and talk to you.'

The soldiers had stopped fighting as soon as they heard Kenneth's voice. They were frightened. They trooped out of the wooden fort and went silently back to their boxes – all but seven of them who were so battered that they couldn't march or gallop.

The next day Kenneth lifted up the lids and looked at his toy soldiers. What a sight they were! Not one of them was whole.

'You're not fit to play soldiers with,' he said. '*You* haven't any arms – and *you* have only one leg – and *you* haven't a helmet – and *you* have a horse that has lost its head. What a dreadful sight you all are! I don't want you for soldiers any more. I shall have you for something else.'

So he took three of them for his railway station and made them porters. Four more he put on his toy farm to look after the hens and the sheep. Five of them he put to live in the doll's house, and one of them had to drive the little toy motor-car. The others he thought would do to act in his toy theatre. Then he threw the cardboard boxes into the waste-paper basket, emptied out his money-box and went out of the nursery.

He bought a great big box of cowboys, some with horses and some without. How the soldiers envied them when they saw Kenneth playing games with them!

'You shouldn't have been so quarrelsome!' said the rabbit. 'It's your own fault that you're stuck away in the farm and the dolls' house, instead of being proper soldiers.'

'We wish we could have another chance!' said the red and green soldiers, looking longingly at the cowboys prancing about the floor on their big horses. But it wasn't any use wishing. They never did have another chance!

THE TALL PINK VASE

Jill and Leslie lived in one of two cottages. The cottages were joined on to one another. One was called Buttercup Cottage and the other was called Daisy Cottage. Jill and Leslie lived in Buttercup Cottage, but Daisy Cottage was empty.

Then one day a furniture van arrived outside Daisy Cottage. The children were very much excited. Hurrah! Someone was coming to live in Daisy Cottage at last!

'I wonder what the people will be like,' said Jill. 'I do hope there will be some children.'

But what a disappointment! There were no children at all. Only a plump little lady with merry, twinkling eyes called Miss Bustle.

'Bother!' said Jill, 'I wish there had been a boy or a girl too.'

'Look at that dreadful pink vase going in,'

55

said Leslie suddenly. 'Oh, Jill! Isn't it an ugly thing!'

Jill looked. It certainly was the ugliest vase she had ever seen. It was a bright pink, very tall and narrow, and had big yellow flowers here and there.

Jill's mother loved flowers and had many lovely vases – green jars, blue bowls and yellow jugs, which the children loved. They had never seen such an ugly thing as the pink vase going into the cottage next door.

'I don't think we shall like that person much if her things are all like that dreadful vase,' said Jill. 'I expect she will have paper flowers instead of real ones, and a china dog instead of a real puppy.'

'And mats that mustn't be dirtied, and cushions you mustn't lean against,' said Leslie. 'I don't think we'll make friends with our new neighbour, Jill.'

'Children, children!' called Mother. 'It's not polite to stare like that. Come away from the wall and play in the garden at the back.'

The children didn't bother any more about Miss Bustle. They went to school, played in the garden, went for walks and took no notice of the cottage next door at all. If they had, they would have seen that Miss Bustle was simply longing to smile at them and talk to them. But they ran by Daisy Cottage without a single look.

Then one day Leslie happened to look at

Daisy Cottage from their back garden and he saw the dreadful pink vase standing at one of the windows.

'Oh, Jill, look! There's that ugly vase again!' he cried.

'Well, I *shan't* look,' said Jill. 'It was quite bad enough the first time. Come on, Leslie, let's play cricket with your new ball.'

'You can bat first,' said Leslie. 'I'll bowl.'

He bowled his new ball to Jill. She missed it and it went into the rose-bed. She found it and sent it back to Leslie. He bowled again.

It was an easy ball. Jill lifted her bat and swiped at it. Crack! She sent the ball right up into the air, spinning over the wall next door in the direction of the upstairs windows. The children watched it in fright. Would it break a window?

No – it struck the tall pink vase that stood at

an open window and broke it in half! Crash! The pieces fell down inside the window. The cricket-ball rolled along the window-ledge and fell outside the window down to the flower-bed below.

The children looked at one another in dismay. Whatever would Miss Bustle say? They waited for her to put her head out of the window – but nothing happened.

'Perhaps she's out,' said Leslie.

'Yes, I remember now – she is,' said Jill. 'I saw her go out with a basket about half an hour ago.'

'Let's go and get our ball,' said Leslie. So they climbed quickly over the wall, found their ball and climbed back. They sat down on the grass and looked at one another.

They were both thinking the same thing. If Miss Bustle was out, perhaps they needn't own up to breaking the vase. She might think the curtain had blown against it and knocked it down.

'Do you think we need say anything?' asked Jill at last.

Leslie went red. 'We *needn't*,' he said. 'But we must, Jill. We'd be cowards not to own up.'

'And, oh, dear, I expect Miss Bustle loves that vase better than anything in the world,' said Jill, with a groan. 'And we'll have to buy another out of our money-box.'

'Look, there she is, coming back,' said Leslie.

'Come on, Jill, let's get it over while we feel brave.'

So they went to the door of Daisy Cottage and knocked. Miss Bustle opened the door and stared at them in surprise.

'Please,' said Leslie, 'we've come to say we're very sorry but our cricket-ball broke your pink vase and if you'll tell us how much it was we'll buy you another.'

'Broken that pink vase!' exclaimed Miss Bustle. 'Have you *really*?'

'I'm afraid so,' said Jill, very red in the face.

'Well, I *am* glad it's broken at last!' said Miss Bustle, in a delighted voice. 'An old friend gave it to me and I've always hated it, but I didn't like to throw it away as it was given to me. I've always hoped it would get broken, it was so very ugly, but somehow it never did. And now at last it's smashed. Oh, dear me, I *am* glad!

59

Come in, do, and have a bun and some lemonade, and see my new puppy. I only brought him home today.'

Well, would you believe it! Jill and Leslie were so surprised and delighted to hear that Miss Bustle, instead of being angry with them, was really pleased! They could hardly believe their ears. They stepped inside and found that Daisy Cottage was the gayest, prettiest, cosiest little place they had ever seen.

She showed them the puppy in his basket and then went out to get the lemonade and buns.

'Isn't it a pretty house?' said Jill to Leslie. 'Not a bit like we imagined. And isn't Miss Bustle nice?'

'You know,' said Miss Bustle, hurrying back with a jug, 'I didn't think you were very nice children. You never spoke to me or smiled. I

thought you were horrid. But now I know better. It was so nice of you to come and own up about the vase, because it *might* have been one I liked. And I can see now that you are nice, bright, smiley children.'

Jill told Miss Bustle how they had seen the pink vase and hated it. 'We *were* silly!' she said. 'We thought you'd be like that vase, so we didn't bother about being good neighbours at all. Do forgive us.'

'Of course, of course,' said Miss Bustle, setting ginger buns in front of them. 'I'd forgive anyone anything if they had broken that horrid pink vase. Do come and see me often. I've got a nephew and niece coming to stay with me soon, so perhaps you would come out for picnics and motor rides with us?'

'Oh, *rather*!' said Jill and Leslie happily. 'Thank you very much!'

Now they are so much in Daisy Cottage with Miss Bustle and the puppy that their mother says she really thinks they ought to live there altogether!

'Wasn't it a good thing we owned up about that broken vase!' Jill often says to Leslie. 'We *should* have missed a lot of fun if we hadn't!'

WHISKERS AND THE PARROT

Whiskers the cat lived with Miss Nellie, and was her great pet. He had a special chair of his own with a special cushion, a china dish with kittens all round it, and a saucer of blue and yellow.

So you can guess that he thought a great deal of himself. The other cats he met out in the garden didn't like Whiskers at all. They thought he was selfish, proud and stuck-up.

'One day you'll have your punishment,' said Tailer, the next-door Tabby. But Whiskers yawned in his face very rudely and didn't even bother to answer.

And then Miss Nellie bought a parrot in a cage! Good gracious me, you should have seen Whiskers' face when he saw the parrot sitting in its cage in a sunny corner of the dining-room. The cage hung from a hook in the ceiling, and the parrot sat in the sun and fluffed out all her feathers.

She saw Whiskers and cocked her grey and red head on one side.

'Hallo, hallo, hallo!' she said.

Whiskers nearly shot out of the room with fright. What was this thing that looked like a big bird and talked like a human being?

'Woof, woof, woof!' said the parrot, pretending to bark like a dog.

Whiskers mewed in fright and ran under the table. He thought there really was a dog in the room.

'Ha-ha, ha-ha, ha-ha!' jeered the parrot. 'Hallo, hallo! Pretty Polly, pretty Polly!'

Just then Miss Nellie came into the room and laughed to see Whiskers under the table.

'Why, Whiskers!' she cried. 'Surely you are not frightened of my Polly parrot? I want you to be friends.'

But that was just what Whiskers was not going to be! As soon as he was used to the parrot and knew that it was only a big bird that could talk, he made up his mind to catch Polly somehow. He would wait until Miss Nellie was safely out of the way and then he would get down that big cage and eat the parrot.

So he waited his time, and at last his chance came. Miss Nellie went out to tea with a friend and left her parrot and her cat shut up in the dining-room together.

'Miaow!' said Whiskers fiercely, looking up at the cage. 'Now I'm going to get you!'

'Pretty Polly, pretty Polly!' cried the parrot, climbing up and down her big cage. 'Hallo, hallo!'

Whiskers crouched to spring up at the cage. He leapt right up in the air and sprang on to the side of the cage. Crash – crash! The hook came out of the ceiling and the cage fell with a loud bang on to the floor!

Whiskers was frightened. He didn't know that his weight would bring the cage down. The parrot was frightened too. Whiskers ran into a corner to hide.

The parrot looked round – and saw that the crash had made the door of the cage fly open. Ha! Now she could get out and fly round a bit!

Out of the cage she hopped and flew up to the top of the curtain. Whiskers watched her in surprise. Perhaps he could get that parrot now.

He crept out from the corner and lay watching, swishing his tail from side to side. The parrot saw the moving tail and suddenly flew down to the table. Before the surprised cat knew what was happening the parrot shot down and nipped his tail hard, right at the tip.

'Miaow!' cried the cat in pain and surprise.

'Ha-ha, ha-ha!' laughed the parrot, sitting on the top of the clock. Whiskers leapt at the big bird, who at once spread her wings and flew to the electric light over the table, screeching loudly as she went. Then it was the parrot's turn. She suddenly flew at Whiskers and pecked him on the nose!

'Miaow!' wailed the cat, and the parrot flew up to the top of a picture, where she screeched and squawked very happily.

Whiskers wondered what to do. Then he thought of a good idea. He would creep into the parrot's cage and lie down there. Perhaps when it was dark the parrot would go back to her cage again and then Whiskers could get her! So as soon as the parrot's back was turned, Whiskers crept into the cage. Polly was happily pulling all the flowers out of a vase and took no notice of Whiskers at all.

Then she looked round to see where the cat was, and when she spied him in the cage how she laughed! In a trice the parrot flew down and shut the door of the cage with a clang. Whiskers was a prisoner!

'Ha-ha, ha-ha!' chuckled the mischievous parrot in glee, and settled down on Whiskers' own cushion, in Whiskers' own chair. Soon Whiskers saw that the parrot was pulling all the fluff out of the cushion!

Whiskers mewed angrily and tried to get out of the cage – but the door was fast shut. Whiskers clawed at the door, but it was no good. He could *not* open it!

And there Miss Nellie found him when she arrived home again. The first thing she saw when she switched on the light was the parrot fast asleep on the curtain-rod. Then she saw the cage on the floor, and to her great surprise, spied Whiskers inside, with the door fast shut!

'O-ho, Whiskers!' she cried. 'So you jumped at the cage and made it fall down, did you? And Polly escaped out of the cage and you got in! And somehow or other the door was shut and made you a prisoner! Well, it serves you right. I shall leave you there for the night, and then, perhaps, you won't even *look* at the parrot-cage again.'

So there poor Whiskers had to stay all night long, and Polly laughed and chuckled, screeched and squawked whenever she thought of him.

The next day the cage was opened and Whiskers crawled out. He ran into the garden, and found that all the cats there had heard what had happened – and how they teased him!

'You won't be so proud now, Whiskers!' they said. 'Who got caught in the parrot-cage? Ho-ho!'

And now Whiskers never takes any notice of the parrot at all, and would never dream of eating it – but Polly hasn't forgotten. She cries: 'Poor pussy, poor pussy!' whenever she sees Whiskers – and he doesn't like it at all!

THE ODD LITTLE BIRD

Once upon a time there was a fine fat hen who was sitting on twelve eggs. Eleven of the eggs were brown but the twelfth was a funny greeny-grey colour. The hen didn't like it very much. She thought it must be a bad egg.

'Still,' she thought to herself, 'I'll see if it hatches out with the others. If it doesn't, well, it will show it is a bad egg.'

After many days the hen was sure her eggs were going to hatch.

'I can hear a little "cheep cheep" in one of them!' she clucked excitedly to all the other hens. Sure enough one of the eggs cracked, and out came a fluffy yellow chick, who cuddled up in the mother-hen's feathers with a cheep of joy.

Then one by one all the other eggs cracked too, and tiny fluffy birds crept out – all except the greeny-grey egg. No chick came from that. It lay there in the nest unhatched.

'Well, I'll give it another day or two,' said the hen, sitting down on it again. 'After that I won't sit on it any more.'

In two days the hen found that the twelfth egg was cracking too. Out came a small bird – but it wasn't a bit like the other chicks!

It was yellow, certainly – but its beak was bigger and quite different. Its body was different too, and the little creature waddled about clumsily instead of running with the others.

The mother hen didn't like it. She pecked it and clucked: 'Oh, you funny-looking little thing! I'm sure you don't belong to me.'

The other chicks didn't like the little waddling bird, either. They called it names and shooed it away when it went to feed with them. It was sad and unhappy, for not even the mother-hen welcomed it or called it to enjoy a tit-bit as she did the others.

'I'm the odd one,' it said to itself. 'I wonder

why? I can't run fast like the others, and I don't look like them either. I am ugly and nobody wants me.'

The odd little bird grew faster than the others, and at last it was so much bigger that the little chicks didn't like to peck it any more, for they were afraid it might peck back and hurt them. So they left it alone, and stopped calling it names.

But the mother-hen was not afraid of it. She was often very cross with it indeed, especially when the rain came and made puddles all over the hen-run.

For then the odd little bird would cheep with delight and go splashing through the puddles in joy.

'You naughty, dirty little creature!' clucked the mother-hen. 'Come back at once. No chicken

likes its feet to be wet. You must be mad, you naughty little thing!'

Then the odd little bird would be well pecked by the hen, and would sit all by itself in a corner, watching the rain come down and wishing it could go out in it.

One day it found a hole in the hen-run and crept through it. Not far off it saw a piece of water, and on it were some lovely white birds, swimming about and making loud quacking noises. Something in the odd little bird's heart cried: 'Oh, if only I could be with those lovely birds, how happy I should be!'

But then it grew sad. 'No,' it said to itself, 'I am a queer, odd little bird. Nobody wants me. But all the same I will just go to the edge of the water and paddle my feet in it. I can run away if those big white birds chase me.'

So off it went and paddled in the water. It was lovely. At first the big white ducks took no notice of the little bird, and then two came swimming up quite near to him.

'Hallo!' they cried. 'What a little beauty you are! Come along with us and have a swim. We'd be proud to have you.'

At first the little bird didn't know that the ducks were talking to him. But when he saw that they really were, he was too astonished to answer. At last he found his voice, and said: 'But, lovely creatures, surely you don't want me, such an odd, ugly little bird as I am!'

'You're not odd or ugly,' cried the ducks. 'You are a beautiful little duck, like us. Come along, it is time you learnt to swim. Don't go back to those funny little chicks any more. Live with us, and have a fine swim on the water!'

The odd little bird could hardly believe what he heard. So he wasn't odd or ugly, after all! He was only different from the chicks because he was a duckling! And he would grow up to be like these lovely white creatures, and swim with them on the water. Oh, what happiness!

'Quack, quack!' he said, for the first time, and swam boldly out to join the ducks. The old mother-hen spied him through the hole in the run and squawked to him to come back. But he waggled his tail and laughed.

'No, no!' he cried. 'You will never make a hen of me. I'm a duck, a duck, a duck!'

THE MECCANO MOTOR-CAR

Tom had made a Meccano motor-car to put Elizabeth's dolls in. It was rather a queer-looking car, but when Elizabeth had put in a few little cushions out of her dolls' house, and sat her dolls in the seat, it looked quite real.

'We shall have to push it along the floor because it won't go like a real car,' said Tom. 'Wait a minute though! Where's my clockwork engine? I know how to take the clockwork out of that, and perhaps I can put it into the Meccano motor-car.'

He tried it – and it worked! He wound up his home-made motor-car and it ran along the floor by itself, taking the dolls with it. Tom and Elizabeth were delighted.

They showed it to Mummy when she came to put them to bed.

'It's very good,' she said. 'Leave it there on the floor, and I'll show it to Daddy when he comes in.'

So they left it there, with all the dolls sitting on the seats. And that night, when everyone was asleep, you should have seen how excited those dolls were! They came alive and called to the sailor doll to wind up the Meccano motor-car to let it take them round and round the nursery again.

'I say!' said the curly-haired doll suddenly, 'Let's call the pixies in! They're holding a party under the lilac bush tonight, and they would so love to see our car.'

So they called to the pixies, and they all came tumbling in at the window in great excitement.

'Let's have a ride, let's have a ride!' they cried, when they saw the motor-car. In they got, and one of the dolls showed them how to steer the little wheel. The pixies soon learnt how to drive, and my goodness me! how they tore

74

about the nursery, almost running over the pink rabbit and nearly knocking down the blue teddy-bear.

They made such a noise that Tom and Elizabeth woke up. They slept in the room next to the nursery, and they sat up in bed and wondered whatever was happening.

'It sounds as if something was tearing about across the nursery floor,' said Tom. 'Whatever can it be?'

'Let's go and look!' said Elizabeth. So they crept out of bed and went to the day-nursery. The moon was shining right into it and they could see everything quite clearly.

And weren't they surprises! They saw their toy motor-car tearing round and round, full of small pixies who were yelling with excitement. The dolls all stood watching, and the blue teddy-bear held up his paw, saying: 'Sh! Sh! Sh! Not so much noise! You'll wake the children!'

Tom and Elizabeth could hardly believe their eyes. They stood peeping in at the door, watching. And as they watched they saw the Meccano motor-car dash straight into a chair. Bump! It turned over and all the pixies fell out.

'Oh, my goodness!' cried Elizabeth, quite forgetting that she didn't mean to be seen.

As soon as she had cried out, all the pixies gave a squeal of fright and flew out of the window. The toys rushed back to the cupboard and sat themselves down at once, keeping as still as could be. The Meccano motor-car didn't move. It lay on its side.

Tom and Elizabeth were just going to step into the nursery when they heard their mother's voice.

'Elizabeth! Tom! Whatever are you doing? Go back to bed at once!'

'But, Mummy, such funny things have been happening in the nursery,' said Tom. 'We saw some fairies riding in the motor-car we made, and all the toys were alive!'

'Oh, nonsense! You were just dreaming,' said Mummy. 'Go back to bed before you get a cold, both of you!'

So to bed they had to go, and they soon fell asleep again. In the morning they looked at one another.

'*Did* we really see those fairies and our toys all alive?' said Elizabeth. 'Or did we dream it?'

'Well, we couldn't *both* have dreamed it, could we?' said Tom. 'We'll see if the motor-car is still lying on its side in the nursery.'

It was! And do you know, tucked in one of

the seats was a tiny silver wand with a shiny star on the end of it! One of the pixies must have left it behind.

'There!' said Elizabeth, in delight. 'It *was* real. We didn't dream it. Oh Tom! Let's use the wand and wish a wish!'

So when they are in bed tonight, they are going to wave that tiny wand and wish a wish. I do wonder what will happen!

THE JUMPING FROG

All the toys in the nursery were perfectly happy before the horrid jumping frog came. They used to play peacefully together, having a lovely time, never quarrelling, never snapping at one another or teasing.

But as soon as the jumping frog came he spoilt everything. For one thing he talked all the time, and for another thing he was always jumping out at the toys and giving them frights.

They couldn't bear him, but they were too polite to say so. They begged him not to frighten them, but he took no notice.

'You don't need to be frightened of *me*!' he would say. 'It's only my fun.'

But it wasn't fun to the toys. The teddy-bear fell over and bumped his nose when the frog jumped out at him from behind the cupboard; and the captain of the wooden soldiers broke his gun through tumbling down in fright when the frog jumped right on top of him.

'One of these days,' said the big humming-top solemnly to the frog, 'one of these days, frog, you will be sorry for all these tricks of yours. People who frighten others always end in getting a terrible fright themselves. And when that happens, *we* shan't help you!'

One night the jumping frog planned to frighten the teddy-bear. The frog could wind himself up, so he was able to jump about whenever he wanted to. He knew that the teddy-bear often walked round by the window at night so he thought he would hide behind the big waste-paper basket and jump out at him as he came walking by. How frightened the golliwog would be! How he would squeak! How fast he would run, and how the jumping frog would laugh!

The frog wound himself up and hid behind the waste-paper basket. He waited and he waited. At last he peeped out. Ah, was that the teddy-bear coming? Yes, it must be. Now for a good high jump to frighten him out of his skin!

The frog jumped – but oh, my goodness me! it wasn't the teddy-bear after all. It was the big black kitchen cat! The jumping frog saw him just as he landed flat on the cat's back.

'Sssssssssss-tt!' hissed the cat angrily, and flashed round to see what it was that had fallen on her back, and was now slipping to the floor.

Out went her paw and gave the jumping frog a good smack. He leapt away in fright. The cat went after him.

All the toys peeped out of the cupboard in surprise. Whatever was happening?

'It's the frog!' cried the teddy-bear. 'He jumped out at the cat, thinking it was me, I expect. And now the cat is chasing him! Oh my, what a fright he is in.'

'Serve him right!' cried the toys.

'Help! Help!' squealed the frog, jumping for all he was worth.

But the toys were far too much afraid of the cat to go to his rescue. Each of them felt that the frog was getting what he deserved, and what he had so often given others – a good fright!

Jump! Jump! Jump! The frog leapt high in the air half a dozen times as the cat went after him. He was so frightened that he didn't look

where he was going and once he nearly jumped right into the fire.

The toys watched, their eyes wide open in surprise. Whatever would happen?

Suddenly the cat shot its claws out at the frog and something clattered to the floor. It was the frog's key, which the cat had clawed out of his back. The frog jumped higher still, frightened almost out of his life. He was near the waste-paper basket, and to the toys' enormous surprise he jumped right into it!

He hadn't meant to − but there he was, at the bottom of the basket, among Nurse's bits of cotton and torn-up paper. And just at that very moment his clockwork ran down. He could jump no more. He couldn't wind himself up, either, because his key had fallen out. There he must stay.

The cat didn't know where the frog had gone. She hunted about for a while and then ran out of the nursery to catch mice in the kitchen. The toys ran to the waste-paper basket and peeped in.

'Help me out,' said the frog. 'I've had such a fright.'

'Serve you right!' said the teddy-bear sternly. 'We can't help you out, the basket is too tall. You'll be emptied into the dust-bin tomorrow, and that will be the end of you. You've always been fond of giving other people frights, so you can't complain of what has happened to *you*!'

The next morning the housemaid took the waste-paper basket downstairs, and emptied it into the dust-bin. The jumping frog went in all among the tea-leaves and potato-peel. He was very unhappy, and wished many times that he had been kind and jolly, instead of unkind and mean.

'I wonder what happened to him in the dust-bin,' said the toys to one another. But no one ever knew!

THE LITTLE BROWN PONY

Monty had a little brown pony for his birthday. It was a pretty little thing, not very tall, with a long brown mane and tail.

Monty wasn't very pleased. 'Pooh!' he said to himself when he saw it. 'Why didn't Dad give me a horse? I don't want a silly little pony! It won't be able to gallop nearly fast enough for me. I'd like a big horse that goes like the wind.'

He didn't say all this to his father, though. No, he didn't dare! His father called Monty to him and spoke gravely to him.

'Now listen, Monty,' he said. 'You are a very lucky boy to have a pony for your birthday, and I want you to be sure to treat it kindly and well.

83

You are not very good with animals, for you let your rabbit die, and you never remembered to take your puppy for a walk when you had one. The gardener will teach you how to look after your pony properly, and you may ride him twice a day, if you wish. And remember, always be kind to him!'

Monty promised, but after a little while he grew bored with having to brush his pony and see to its water and food. He found that it couldn't go fast enough for him and soon he began to whip it and shout at it. The little thing was frightened and did its best for Monty, but he was impatient and unkind.

The small girl who lived next door to Monty often used to watch him riding the pony. She had always wanted a pony of her own, but her Daddy couldn't afford one. So she watched Monty's pony instead, and sometimes she would climb over the wall and go to help the gardener groom the pretty little animal.

'Do you like doing that sort of work?' asked Monty scornfully one day, watching Ann brush his pony till its coat gleamed and shone.

'Yes, I do,' said Ann. 'I wish I could do it always. I love your little pony, Monty.'

'Well, look here – if you'll look after my pony for me, I'll let you ride it once a week,' said Monty. 'I hate looking after it. It's a silly animal, anyway. I want a great big horse that will gallop!'

Ann promised to care for his pony each day, and once a week Monty let her have a short ride on it. Ann grew very fond of the pony, and the fonder she grew the more she hated seeing Monty whip the little animal and shout at it.

'You shouldn't do that,' she said to him. 'It's

unkind.'

'Hold your tongue!' said Monty rudely. 'Whose pony is this, yours or mine? I shall do what I like with it!'

The pony grew frightened of Monty and one day when the boy galloped it round and round the field, slashing it with a big stick, the pony lost its temper. It stood quite still and wouldn't move a step. Ann was watching over the wall, and she shouted to Monty to jump off.

'Stop it, Monty!' she called. 'The pony is getting angry.'

'What do I care!' cried Monty, and he hit the pony hard. It suddenly galloped off, nearly

throwing Monty, and rushed for the open gate
that led into the road. Ann saw that it was
running away with Monty. In a trice she was
over the wall, and reached the gate just as the
pony got there. She caught hold of the reins and
dragged at them with all her strength.

The pony stopped just outside the gate, and
Monty slid off. Ann's arms were almost pulled
out of her shoulders.

'You're a cruel boy!' she said, through her
tears. 'You don't deserve to be saved when the
pony's running away. I wish *I* had him! I'd love
him and be kind to him. You don't like him a
bit. You don't even look after him. I do all that!'

'What's all this?' said a deep voice, and who
should look over the hedge at the other side of
the road but Monty's father. 'Ann, I saw what
you did. You're a brave little girl, and I'm proud
of you. As for Monty, I'm thoroughly ashamed
of him. I saw him lashing the pony and I don't
wonder it ran away.'

Monty's father led the pony back to its stable and there he heard from the gardener how Ann looked after it each day, and how all that Monty did was to ride it and whip it every day. Monty's father looked very stern. 'Very well,' he said to Monty. 'You have disobeyed me. Now you must be punished. As Ann loves the pony and looks after it so well, she shall have it for her own. You don't deserve to go riding at all, and you are never to ride the pony again. It's Ann's now.'

Well, what do you think of that? Ann was so overjoyed that she could hardly say a word. Monty turned red and ran off. The pony gave a little whinny of delight and snuggled its nose into the small girl's hand.

'I'm happy now!' whinnied the pony.

'So am I!' cried Ann. 'We'll have *lovely* times together!' They do, too – you should just see them galloping round the field on a sunny morning! As for Monty, he always looks the other way.

THE MOST SURPRISING
CHAIR

Once there was a lazy child called Susan. She wouldn't get up in the morning, she wouldn't hurry herself to dress, and even in the daytime she would flop down into an armchair and stay there till her mother tipped her out.

She was always late for morning school, and her teacher scolded her hard. But when she began to be late for afternoon school as well, her teacher wondered whatever was the matter.

'Well, you see,' explained Susan, 'I do feel so sleepy after my dinner that I curl up in an armchair and fall asleep. When I wake up I'm late. My mother won't bother about me any more, so I'm afraid I shall always be late!'

Now the armchair that Susan curled up in after her after dinner was an old, old one. It loved people to sit in it, and it was good to old people and made itself as comfy as possible for them.

But it really couldn't bear lazy people, and when Susan, who was young and strong, curled up in it so lazily every day, the old chair grumbled away to itself and tried to make its seat as hard and as uncomfortable as it could.

But it wasn't a bit of use. Susan didn't even notice it was hard. She went off to sleep at once! She always ate too much at dinner-time and this made her very sleepy.

The chair creaked loudly. Susan didn't wake. The chair made its seat as hard as wood and its arms like iron. Susan didn't stir. The school bell rang loudly. Susan slept peacefully on. And this happened every afternoon. Wasn't it dreadful!

Susan's mother was so tired of scolding her that she no longer bothered to wake her up.

'You can be punished for your lazy ways at school,' she said. 'I can't be bothered with you any more.'

But the old chair grew more and more angry. It worked itself up to such a state that one afternoon a most peculiar thing happened.

Susan had eaten a big plate of meat-pie and had had three helpings of treacle pudding. She felt very sleepy and even snored a little.

This was too much for the chair. It gave an angry creak and then another. It shook itself. It lifted up a foot and tapped loudly on the floor.

Susan slept on! The chair tapped with another foot. Susan snored gently. Oh, naughty Susan, wake up, before anything happens!

The chair lost its temper.

'I've four feet and four legs. I can walk on them as well as stand on them. I'll take this lazy child to school and see what she says when she wakes up there!'

And with that the chair lifted up first one leg, then another – and soon it was walking out of the room, making a clip-clop noise on the floor as it went.

Susan slept peacefully on. The chair went into the hall. The front door was open, and the postman was just putting a letter on the mat. He saw the chair, gave a frightened shout and rushed off! The chair gave a creak and went out of the front door.

Well, as soon as it was in the street, with people walking near, everyone stopped in surprise. They stared at the chair, they nudged one another when they saw the sleeping Susan, and they looked half frightened. But nobody tried to stop the chair until it met Mr. Plod the policeman.

He saw the chair coming towards him and looked most astonished. When it came near him, making a clip-clop noise with its feet on the pavement, he cleared his throat politely – 'er-hurrrrrr!' – and put up his hand.

'Stop!' he said. But the chair took no notice at all. It just gave a loud and rather rude creak, and went under the policeman's hand. Mr Plod was annoyed. He took out his notebook and ran after the chair.

'Are you a new kind of motorcar?' he cried. 'Where's your licence? You haven't got a number-plate!'

He saw the chair, gave a frightened shout and rushed off

The chair creaked again and set off so fast that the policeman was soon left behind. It bumped into Mrs Hurry and gave her a dreadful shock. It trod on Mr Toppy's foot and made him hop about in pain, and he shouted in surprise to see such a curious sight as an armchair hurrying by with a little girl fast asleep in it.

At last the armchair reached the school. The children had all gone in, but the door was still a little open. The teacher was calling the children's names to see that they were all in time.

'Alice! Ben! Mary! Mollie! Eric!'

'Here, Miss Brown. Here, Miss Brown,' answered the children politely, as their names were called.

And then Miss Brown came to Susan's name. 'Susan!' she called – at the very moment the door opened and in came the armchair with Susan!

'Look! Look!' shrieked all the children. 'Susan's in time – the chair has brought her! She's fast asleep – oh, she's fast asleep!'

They all began to laugh loudly as they gathered round the creaking armchair, which was now standing still by Miss Brown's desk.

Susan awoke, for the noise was really almost deafening. She rubbed her eyes and looked around.

'Oh!' she said. 'Where am I? I've been asleep! How did I come to school?'

'The armchair brought you, the armchair

brought you!' shouted the children, dancing round in delight. 'It was awake, and it brought you by itself! Oh, what a funny thing, Susan!'

Susan was ashamed. She got out of the armchair and ran to her desk. She sat down, very red.

When the chair saw Susan safely at her desk it gave a creak as if to say goodbye, and clip-clopped to the door. It squeezed out and clip-clopped home, taking no notice of anyone. Susan had got to school in time for once!

Well, do you know, Susan got teased so much about the chair bringing her to school, and was so afraid that perhaps her bed might play her the same trick in the morning, that she quite turned over a new leaf. Now she is up as soon as her mother calls her, and she never dares to go to sleep after dinner.

So she isn't late for school any more and has got as many good marks as anyone. But if the chair sees her yawning, you should hear it creak.

'Cr-eeeeeeeeeak!' it goes. And Susan stops yawning at once and gets some work to do. Poor old Susan! She never sits in that old armchair any more, as you can guess!

THE BOY WHO THREW STONES

Once upon a time there was a boy called
Sammy. He could throw and catch very well
indeed, so he was a good cricketer, and fine at
ball games.

He could throw stones very well too. If you
drove a nail lightly into a tree-trunk, Sammy
could stand quite a good way off, throw a stone
and hit the tiny nail so hard that it was driven
into the tree!

Sammy was proud of his throwing. But he
didn't only throw stones at marks in trees and
things like that – he threw them at birds, cats,
and dogs. And because he was such a good shot
he always hit them.

The other boys and girls couldn't bear to see
birds and animals hurt.

'Please don't throw stones, Sammy,' they begged. But Sammy laughed.

'The birds and animals should get out of the
way more quickly!' he said, and threw a stone
at a cat asleep on the wall. The stone hit her
on the back and she woke up with a loud mew
of pain.

Now one little girl had a great-grandmother

who looked like a kindly old witch with twinkling eyes and a mouth that was always smiling.
Ellie, the little girl, used to visit her Great-
Granny every Friday, after school, and she
made up her mind to tell her about Sammy.

'Perhaps Great-Granny can stop him from
being so unkind,' she thought. 'I'll ask her.'

So, when she was sitting down to a fine tea
of bread and honey, chocolate cake and ginger
biscuits, Ellie told Great-Granny about Sammy.

'You see, Great-Granny,' she said, 'he's so
proud of being a good shot that he throws stones
at all the birds and animals he sees. And oh,
Great-Granny, he broke a robin's leg the other
day. It made me cry to see it.'

Great-Granny's mouth looked rather stern.

'A boy who can do that needs a lesson,' she
said, and her kind eyes stopped twinkling.

'That's what I thought,' said Ellie, eating a
ginger biscuit and staring at her Great-Granny.
'I wondered if *you* knew how to teach him a
lesson, Great-Granny. You are so old and wise,
aren't you?'

'I might be able to,' said Great-Granny. 'I
will think about it. Now, eat your tea and don't
worry any more about Sammy.'

So Ellie ate her tea and talked about her tortoise, which was getting sleepy. Ellie thought
she ought to put it in a box to sleep for the
winter.

All the time that Great-Granny was talking

to Ellie about her tortoise she was thinking how she might teach Sammy a lesson. And at last she thought of a way. Then she smiled, and Ellie wondered what made Great-Granny rub her hands together in glee all of a sudden.

After Ellie had gone, Great-Granny took a sheet of paper and wrote something on it. She pinned it up on the fence outside her front garden, ready for Sammy to see when he came by. Then she went indoors and made a strange mixture which she poured into a lemonade jug.

Now, when Sammy came by that way, it was Saturday morning, and there was no school. He was whistling as he walked, and held in his hand some small stones ready to throw at anything he saw. When he saw the notice outside Ellie's Great-Granny's house, he stopped and read it. This is what it said:

TO ALL GOOD THROWERS
A THROWING MATCH
WILL BE HELD AFTER TEA TODAY.
WALK IN AND TRY YOUR LUCK

'Oooh!' said Sammy. 'Good! I'll certainly go in for this throwing match. How lucky I came this way and saw the notice!'

So, after tea that day, with his pocket full of smooth stones, Sammy walked in Great-Granny's front gate and knocked at her door. She opened it.

'Ah! A thrower!' she said. 'Come in, come in!'

Sammy went in. He looked round. Nobody else seemed to be there.

'Will you have a drink of lemonade?' asked Great-Granny, and she poured him out a glass of the strange mixture she had made. Sammy drank it. It was very sweet, and he thought it was nice, but not a bit like lemonade.

'Sit down in this chair,' said Great-Granny, and Sammy sat down. He felt very sleepy. He blinked and he blinked. Suddenly he heard another knock at the door. Great-Granny opened it, and to Sammy's enormous surprise, two dogs came in walking on their hind legs, talking to one another.

Sammy sat up and stared. Could he be dreaming? Before he could make up his mind there came another knock, and this time three cats came in, also walking on their hind legs, chattering away gaily. Then three hens ran in on long legs, and two ducks. Then with a rush, came a crowd of smaller birds – blackbirds, thrushes, sparrows, and robins. One of the robins had its leg bandaged all the way up.

'I can't make this out,' said Sammy to Great-Granny, who was busy welcoming everyone. 'You don't seem surprised to see all these animals and birds coming in like this! But it seems very astonishing to me.'

'Oh, it's the throwing match that has brought

them,' said Great-Granny. 'We'll begin in a minute.'

'Are these creatures going in for the throwing match as well as me?' asked Sammy, still more surprised.

'Of course,' said Great-Granny. 'Now then everyone, let's go out and begin.'

She opened the back door and everyone trooped out. But instead of there being a little back garden there was a field! At one end were piles of little stones. At the other end there was a place marked for the target.

Sammy was more and more surprised. He stared and stared. A large cock began to crow. Everyone fell silent.

'Ladies and gentlemen,' said the cock in a loud voice, 'the match is about to begin. If anyone thinks he is the cleverest thrower here, let him step forward and say so.'

Sammy at once stepped forward. 'I think I must be the cleverest here,' he said. 'I never miss what I throw at!'

All the animals and birds began to talk at once.

'He's right! He never misses!' cried a big brown dog. 'He threw four stones at me one day and hit me with every one!'

'And he threw a stone at me whilst I was singing in a tree, and hit me on the wing,' said a big blackbird.

'Well, you should have seen him throw at *me*!' cried a duck. 'I was the other side of the farmyard, and he threw a stone and hit me all that distance away! He's a marvellous thrower!'

Sammy went red with pleasure. To think that everyone was praising him like this!

'He threw a stone at me and broke my little leg,' said a robin, showing his bandaged leg. 'I was on the fence at the bottom of his garden and he threw a stone from his bedroom window. Oh, yes, he's a very good shot indeed.'

'Well, as he's such a good shot, I don't think we need to ask Sammy to show us what he can do,' said Great-Granny. 'He seems never to miss at all. The thing to do is for you each to have a turn, and we will make Sammy the judge. You shall be the target, Sammy, and tell us if anyone hits you with all his stones.'

'What! Let everyone throw at *me*!' said Sammy, hardly believing his ears.

'Why not?' said Great-Granny. 'You can tell very easily then who is a good shot and who isn't, can't you? If a stone hits you, you can shout "Well thrown!" and if it misses you can shout "Bad shot!"'

'But I shall be hurt!' said Sammy.

'What does that matter?' said Great-Granny. 'All these other creatures were hurt when you practised your throwing, weren't they? Well, if you practise on them, why shouldn't they practise on you? Come, come, Sammy, do as you would be done by. If you expect the animals and birds to let you throw at *them*, you must also allow them to throw stones at *you*!'

All the creatures hustled Sammy to the post which was to be the target at which they all must throw.

'Now don't you dare to run away,' said a big tabby-cat. 'If you do, we shall come after you and scratch you and bite you. Don't spoil our throwing match.'

Sammy stood by the post, trembling. He was afraid. It was one thing to throw stones at others – but quite a different thing to have stones thrown at *him*! He didn't like it at all.

'Tabby-cat, you can take three stones and try first,' said the cock. So the tabby picked up three small pebbles and aimed carefully. Ping! The stone flew through the air and hit Sammy smartly on the ankle.

'Oooh! Ow!' yelled Sammy. 'Don't!'

'Good shot!' shrieked everyone in delight. The tabby cat was delighted. She threw her two other stones, but neither of them hit Sammy. Then it was the turn of the large brown dog. He picked up a pebble and aimed carefully.

Ping! It hit Sammy on the hand. He hopped about, yelling, rubbing first his ankle and then his hand.

'Don't! Don't!' he cried. 'I don't like it! It's unkind!'

'Well, it's what *you* did to us!' yelled back everyone. The dog threw again. His second stone went wide, but his third one hit Sammy on the knee. How he shouted!

The animals and birds laughed. This was a fine throwing match. *They* had been Sammy's target in the past – and now he was theirs! A blackbird took his three stones and aimed carefully.

He was not a good shot and all three of his stones missed. Sammy was so thankful – but it was a different thing when a brown hen ran up and threw. My goodness, she was a good thrower. Her legs were strong with scratching around the farmyard, and she threw hard and straight.

Ping! She got Sammy on his nose. Ping! Another stone hit him on the neck. Ping! The last one hit him sharply on his wrist. Everyone clapped and shouted.

'Oh, good shot, hen, good shot!' But Sammy yelled and hopped around, and then made up his mind to beg for mercy.

'Let me off! Let me off!' he begged. 'I will never throw stones at anything again. I didn't know it hurt so much.'

'You had your fun with us, and now we want ours with you!' shouted back the animals and birds, and they all rushed to take stones at once. That was too much for Sammy. He gave a frightened yell and tore off for home. He ran and he ran, with all the animals and birds after him. He panted and puffed, and was afraid his legs would give way.

He ran and he ran with all the animals and birds after him

At last he saw someone in the distance and he ran towards her as fast as he could, 'Save me! Save me!' he begged, flinging his arms round the surprised person. It was Ellie, going for a walk in the fields!

Ellie stared in astonishment. 'What do you want me to save you from?' she asked. 'There's no one near that I can see.'

Sammy turned round and looked. Sure enough, there wasn't a sign of any animal or bird to be seen.

'Oh, Ellie, I've had such a dreadful time,' said Sammy. 'I saw a notice outside your Great-Granny's about a throwing match – and I went in for it – but all the birds and animals began to throw at *me* and I'm bruised all over. Look!'

'Well, Sammy, I'm sorry for you, but after all your leg isn't broken like that poor little robin's was the other day,' said Ellie. 'It's a funny tale you are telling me. I can hardly believe it is true.'

'Well, come and see the notice outside your Great-Granny's house,' said Sammy. 'Then you'll believe me.'

So they went to see it – but there was no notice there at all! 'You must have been dreaming, Sammy!' said Ellie – though she felt sure it was really her Great-Granny who had managed to teach Sammy a lesson.

'Well, dream or no dream, I'm never going to throw stones at any creature again,' said

Sammy, and he took every stone from his pockets and threw them on the ground.

'Good,' said Ellie. 'It's worth a few bruises to have learnt something like that, Sammy.'

And what about Sammy now? That was last autumn, and Sammy has never thrown another stone at anything. And whenever he passes Ellie's Great-Granny's cottage and sees the old woman there, he is very polite indeed. You never know what a wise old woman like that will do next!

THE BAD LITTLE BOY

Once there was a bad little boy called Jo. He was so bad that he was always getting into trouble and being smacked and sent to bed.

He always got as dirty as could be as soon as he had clean clothes on. He always tore his coat as soon as his mother had bought him a new one. He never remembered to wash behind his ears, and as for remembering to wipe his feet or say please and thank you, well, he really didn't seem able to!

His mother was quite in despair. 'I shall ask your father to deal with you now, Jo,' she said. 'I can't manage you any more.'

Well, Jo's father had one way of dealing with him that Jo didn't like at all. Do you know what it was? He spanked him well with a slipper!

Now Jo grew to hate those slippers of his father's. There they sat, warming by the fire every evening, and Jo knew quite well that if he had been naughty, they were waiting to spank him! So he hated them and wished he could get rid of them.

And one evening he took them away when nobody was looking. He tucked them under his arm, ran upstairs with them and locked them into his cupboard where nobody would find them. Wasn't he a bad little boy?

Well, his father couldn't *think* what had happened to his slippers when he came home that night! Jo's mother scurried here and there looking for them, and Jo himself pretended to hunt too, though all the time the bad little boy was chuckling to himself, knowing that they were safely locked in the cupboard upstairs.

But, dear me, when Jo was in bed that night, a strange thing happened. The slippers wanted to get out of the cupboard! They were cold there, for they were used to warming themselves by the fire when they were not on Jo's Daddy's feet. So they began to stir about in the cupboard, muttering angrily.

'Let us out! We're cold! We're cold!'

Jo sat up and listened. Whatever was that noise? It came from the cupboard. Could he have shut the cat in there by mistake?

'Let us out! Let us out!' cried the two cold slippers.

'Good gracious! Whatever is it?' thought Jo. 'Who is it in the cupboard?' he asked aloud.

'Your father's slippers! We're cold! Let us out!'

'Daddy's slippers! But slippers can't talk!' said Jo.

'Of course we can talk. We've got tongues, haven't we!' said the slippers, and they began to bang at the door.

Jo was frightened. If they made a noise like that they would wake his Mummy and Daddy, and they would find the slippers there and be very angry with him. Whatever was he to do?

'Let us out!' shouted the slippers, Bang, bang! 'Let us out!' Bang, bang, bang!

Jo slipped out of bed quickly. He unlocked the cupboard door and the slippers flapped out. They hopped into Jo's bed.

'Oh no, you can't come there,' said Jo, getting into his warm bed. He threw the slippers out on the floor. 'I'm not having you in bed with me, you nasty, horrid things!'

'Let's spank him, shall we?' said one slipper to the other. Jo listened in alarm. The slippers jumped onto the bed and cuddled down beside Jo under the sheet, where it was warm. Jo didn't dare to turn them out again. They dug themselves well into him and went to sleep. Poor Jo didn't sleep for a long time, for he was very worried over this strange happening.

He always had to make his own bed in the morning, so he left the slippers sleeping peacefully there, and made his bed carefully so that they didn't show. Then he went down to breakfast, not late for once. He was so quiet that his mother wondered if he was ill.

Jo was quiet because he was thinking of some way to get rid of those dreadful slippers. At last he smiled and rubbed his hands. Gardener had a bonfire burning in the garden this week. He would stuff the slippers there after tea and that would be the end of them!

So, after tea, when no one was looking, the bad little boy slipped down to the bonfire with the sleepy slippers. He stuffed them hard into the heart of the bonfire and then skipped back joyfully to the house. That was the end of those annoying slippers!

But, you know, it wasn't! For, in the middle of the night, Jo heard something rapping at the window. He sat up. Then the moon shone into his room, and there, on the window-sill, he could quite clearly see those two slippers.

'Let us in! Let us in!' shouted the slippers angrily. 'We won't be left out on the rubbish-heap! Let us in!'

Well, poor Jo simply *had* to let them in, of course, for he was afraid they would wake up the whole house! So he opened the window and in they jumped, smelling strongly of the bonfire, and rather scorched about the toes.

'You're a bad boy,' said the slippers. 'If that fire hadn't gone out when the rain came, we might have been burnt. Let us come into your warm bed and cuddle down.'

Jo had to let them. He tried to leave them as little room as possible, but those slippers dug their toes into him and squeezed him right to the wall. He was very uncomfortable, and how cross he felt when the slippers began to snore!

'Horrid, nasty things!' he thought. 'I'll get rid of them tomorrow without fail. I'll drown them in the river!'

So the next day, when he had a chance, Jo took the slippers out of his bed, tucked them under his coat and ran down to the river.

'Where are you going?' squeaked the slippers, frightened.

'To drown you!' said Jo. 'Then you won't spank me any more, or creep into my warm bed at night.'

'Oh, yes we will,' said the slippers – but they couldn't say a word more because Jo flung them into the water – splash! The slippers sank at once, and Jo ran home, whistling with glee. He had got rid of them at last.

But alas for poor Jo! In the middle of the night, as he was dreaming peacefully, there came a tap-tap-tapping at his window once again.

'Let us in, you naughty boy! Let us in!' cried the voices of the two slippers.

Jo sat up and groaned. 'Go away,' he said. 'I thought I'd drowned you.'

'Well, you didn't,' said the slippers. 'We just walked over the bottom of the river and crept out. But we are very wet and cold, and we want to get into your bed.'

Jo was full of horror – what, have those wet slippers in his nice, dry, warm bed! Never!

So he lay down again and tried to go to sleep.

But the slippers tap-tapped at the window till Jo thought they would break it.

'We'll go and tap at your father's window,' said the slippers. 'Yes, we will! And we'll tell him what you have done to his favourite slippers these last two days.'

Jo got up. It was no use, he must let those slippers in. So he opened the window and in they came. My goodness, they *were* wet! They made puddles on the carpet as they hopped over to the bed. They jumped in under the sheet and snuggled down warmly.

'This is fine,' they said sleepily. 'This is just what we want. We were afraid of getting a chill.'

Jo got into bed too. The slippers pressed close to him, and his pyjamas got wet and cold. He squeezed himself against the wall – but the slippers came after him and cuddled him close. Jo could not bear it. He felt so wet and cold.

He got out of bed, shivering. He put on his dressing-gown, took the eiderdown, wrapped it round him, and tried to go to sleep in the chair. But it was difficult.

The next day Jo looked white and tired.

'Dear me, Jo!' said his mother, quite worried, 'You look as if you are going to have a cold. You had better stay away from school and have a nice lazy day in bed.'

Now usually this would have pleased Jo very much, for he was lazy. But today he thought of those awful wet slippers in his bed and he didn't want to stay at home at all.

'Oh, I'm quite all right, Mummy,' he said quickly. 'I don't feel at all like going to bed.'

His father was pleased. He looked up from his paper. 'Good boy!' he said. 'I like to see a boy wanting to go to school instead of lazing in bed.'

Jo was pleased. It wasn't often his father found anything to praise, for Jo was usually such a bad little boy. It was nice to find someone talking kindly to him after the way those horrid slippers spoke. He went off to school feeling a bit happier.

What was he to do with those slippers? It wasn't a bit of use trying to get rid of them, for they would only come back in the middle of the night and want to get into his nice warm bed. And Jo had quite made up his mind that he was NOT going to sleep with them any more.

'But what I am I to do?' thought the little boy. 'I really don't know. I don't want those slippers living with me all my life. How I wish I hadn't taken them!'

Then a thought came into his head. Suppose he told his father what had happened? No – that wouldn't do. His father would never, never believe that slippers could talk or walk by themselves.

'Well, suppose I put the slippers back in their place by the fire?' thought Jo. 'I could say I had found them upstairs. If only Mummy and

Daddy would believe me I'd tell them all about the slippers, but they wouldn't. I know what I'll do. I'll tell Daddy honestly that I hid them because I didn't want to be spanked. Then, if he is angry and spanks me, I must put up with it. It will be better than having to sleep with those unkind slippers, anyhow.'

So he went to fetch the slippers. They were in his bed, awake, sneezing a little now and again because they had caught a cold in the river.

'Where are you taking us now?' they cried.

'I'm going to put you downstairs by the fire,' said Jo firmly. 'And I'm going to tell Daddy how I hid you.'

'Oooh!' said the slippers. 'Fancy you daring to do that! Well, we shall like to go back there again. It's nice and warm by the fire. And if we get a bit cold at any time we can always warm ourselves by spanking you when you do anything bad.'

'If you think I'm going to let you spank me again you're mistaken!' said Jo. 'If I have to be good for the rest of my life, I will – but you are never, never going to spank me again, you nasty, horrid pair of slippers!'

He took them downstairs and put them by the fire. How surprised Daddy was to see them again! Jo went red and spoke up.

'Daddy, I hated those slippers because they spanked so hard, so I took them and hid them.

But now I'm sorry I did so. I've brought them back for you. Please forgive me.'

'Well, Jo, it was brave and good of you to own up,' said Daddy, surprised. 'I certainly shan't spank you. I'm proud of you for telling me. Good boy!'

Jo was happy. It was nice to be in his father's good books. He made a face at the slippers. One of them sneezed.

'Oh, Jo, was that you sneezing?' said his mother anxiously. 'I hope you're not getting a cold.'

'Sounds as if the sneeze came from my slippers, dear,' said Daddy, laughing. 'But that couldn't be of course. I expect it was the cat.'

Well, you'll be glad to know that those slippers have never spanked Jo again. He made up his mind to be good and he was, though his father and mother could never understand what changed him. As for those slippers, they are getting old but they still warm themselves by the fire. And if Jo makes a face at them now and again, I really don't blame him, do you?

THE TELL-TALE BIRD

There was once a little girl called Tilly, who told tales all day long. I don't like tell-tales, do you? Well, nobody liked Tilly!

'Mummy, Peter pushed me today! Mummy, Ann dirtied her frock! Mummy, Pussy has been lying on your best cushion! Mummy, the postman dropped one of your letters in the mud and dirtied it – I saw him!'

That was how Tilly told tales all the day, and people got so cross with her! Ah, but wait! She didn't know the tell-tale bird was about!

It came one day and flew in at Tilly's window as she brushed her hair before breakfast. It was a blue and yellow bird with rather a long tail. And it looked very queer because it had ears! No bird has ears like those that animals have, but this bird had feathery ones on each side of its head.

'Shoo!' said Tilly, waving her brush at the bird. 'Shoo! Go away! Birds are not allowed in the house.'

'I am!' squawked the bird in a loud voice. 'I am! I'm the tell-tale bird, I am! And I've been looking for a little girl like you for a long time!

Yes, a long, long time! I've come to live with you. We ought to be friends, Tilly, for you're a tell-tale girl and I'm a tell-tale bird.'

Tilly didn't know what to make of it at all. She decided to tell her mother about the bird when she went downstairs. So down she went – and the bird flew onto her shoulder as she went.

'Mummy, Mummy, this horrid bird flew in my window!' said Tilly, in her usual grumbling voice.

'Tilly didn't brush her hair properly, Tilly didn't brush her hair properly!' squawked the bird, jumping up and down on Tilly's shoulder in a most annoying way.

'Why, it's a tell-tale bird!' said Mummy, in surprise. 'I didn't think there were any left nowadays. Well, Tilly, you'll have to put up with it, I'm afraid, for as long as you tell tales the bird will want to stay with you and be friends.'

Tilly pushed it off her shoulder angrily. 'Nasty thing!' she said. 'Get away! I won't have you here.'

The bird flew to the electric light and swung there on the cord.

'Tilly's got dirty nails!' he squawked. 'Tilly's got dirty nails.'

Tilly was sent to scrub her nails. The bird went with her. The little girl banged the door and wouldn't let the bird come in. But it flew down the stairs, out of the door, and in at the bedroom window. So Tilly had to put up with it.

They went downstairs again together, the bird on Tilly's shoulder. It dug its claws in if Tilly tried to push if off, so she decided it had better stay. But she didn't mean it to come to school with her. Oh dear, no!

They had breakfast. The tell-tale bird had very bad manners and often snatched at something that Tilly was just going to put into her mouth. It made her jump too, whenever it gave a loud squawk, which it always seemed to be doing.

'Tilly's spilt her milk!' squawked the bird, in delight, when it saw Tilly spill a tiny little drop. 'Dirty girl! She's a dirty girl!'

'You horrid tell-tale!' said Tilly, nearly in tears.

'Tilly's hidden her crust under her plate!' squawked the bird in a little while. 'She's a naughty girl!'

'It's only because I've got two teeth loose and I can't chew properly!' cried Tilly, in a rage.

'Well, say so then,' said her daddy. 'Don't hide things and hope we won't notice. That is not at all a brave thing to do.'

'Tilly's a coward, a coward, a coward!' screamed the bird joyously. Tilly got up from the table in tears, and said she was going to get ready for school. The bird went with her. As soon as they were upstairs, Tilly got hold of the bird, smacked it hard, and pushed in into her toy cupboard. She locked the door, got her hat, and tore off to school without even kissing Mummy goodbye. That shows how upset she was!

She was so glad to be rid of the horrid tell-tale bird. She took her place in her class and opened her books. It was sums. She peeped over at the next child's book.

'Billy's got a sum down all wrong, Miss Brown,' she said. 'He's copied it out wrong.'

There was a squawk at the window. There sat the tell-tale bird, its ears cocked up at each side of its head! It had made such a noise in the toy cupboard that Mummy had had to let it out – and it had flown joyfully off to school. As soon as it got there and heard Tilly telling tales as usual, it knew it had found the right little girl.

'Tilly's got a hole in her stocking!' squawked the bird, jigging up and down in delight. 'I saw it this morning. And she had to be sent back at breakfast time to brush her hair again and scrub her dirty nails!'

Tilly went red. The other children giggled. 'Good gracious!' said Miss Brown. 'A tell-tale bird! I haven't seen one for a very long time. Does it belong to you, Tilly?'

'No,' said Tilly, in a rude voice.

'Oh, I do, I do!' cried the bird, flying to Tilly's shoulder and nuzzling its head against her cheek. 'I'm Tilly's tell-tale bird! She's a lovely

"Tilly's got a hole in her stocking!" squawked the bird

tell-tale! I love her, I do!'

'Well, do you mind sitting on the mantelpiece for a bit?' asked Miss Brown. 'I really don't think Tilly can work properly with you on her shoulder.'

'Oh, with pleasure!' cried the bird, and it flew to the mantelpiece, where it looked in a kindly manner at everyone in the class. It was really a most extraordinary bird.

The class worked hard. Suddenly the little boy beside Tilly whispered to the little girl on his other side. At once Tilly put up her hand.

'Miss Brown, Billy's talking and you said we weren't to!' she said.

Miss Brown was just going to say, 'Don't tell tales!' when the tell-tale bird gave a tremendously loud squawk and cried, 'Tilly's got ink on her fingers! Dirty girl! Dirty girl!'

'Be quiet, you horrid creature!' cried Tilly, trying to rub the ink off her fingers.

'Well, Tilly, you can't blame the bird for doing what you do all day long,' said Miss Brown. 'You tell tales – and the bird does too! It is only doing what you do.'

Nothing more happened till the children went out to play. The bird went to sleep with its head under its wing. Tilly was glad. The children went out into the garden and the bird woke up and went too. Soon Tilly came running in.

'Miss Brown, Miss Brown, Tommy pushed Eileen over! And Dick pulled my hair! And Alice dropped her cake on the ground and then picked it up and ate the dirty pieces.'

The tell-tale bird flew onto Tilly's shoulder and flapped its wings in her face.

'Miss Brown, Miss Brown!' it cried, in a voice very like Tilly's. 'Tilly pushed Leslie! And she trod on George's toe on purpose – I saw her! And she fell down and dirtied her clean dress!'

'Dear me!' said Miss Brown. 'Well, Tilly, if I listen to your tales, I must listen to the bird's too.'

'You're not to listen to the horrid tales the bird tells!' cried Tilly, and she rushed out, crying. She made up her mind not to tell a single tale more that morning. The funny thing is that she didn't! The bird went to sleep again, its head under its wing. School was very happy and peaceful.

Tilly ran home, leaving the bird fast asleep on the mantelpiece. Nobody seemed to remember it, not even Miss Brown. Tilly was pleased. She washed her hands, brushed her hair, and sat down at the dinner-table.

'Well, did you have a nice morning, Tilly?' asked Mummy.

'Yes,' said Tilly. 'But a lot of the children were naughty, Mummy. Billy copied his sum down wrong – and Alice got her spelling wrong – and . . .'

The tell-tale bird suddenly flew in at the window with such a loud squawk that Tilly dropped her spoon in fright.

'Here we are again!' said the bird, cocking its feathery ears up straight. 'Tilly fell down and dirtied her dress at playtime! Tilly got ink on her fingers! Tilly told tales! Tilly . . .'

'Be quiet!' shouted Tilly, and she threw her spoon at the bird. It caught it neatly in its beak, and then flew to the table. It dipped the spoon into Tilly's plate of meat, potato, and gravy and began to eat solemnly. Tilly was angry.

'Now listen, Tilly,' said her mother. 'You will have to put up with the tell-tale bird. It only comes to people who tell tales, and it is your own fault that it has come to you. Stop telling tales, and the bird will soon go somewhere else!'

'I'll never tell another tale in my life!' wept Tilly.

But although she had made up her mind about this, she found it was much more difficult than she had thought. She was such a dreadful little tell-tale that it was very difficult for her to stop suddenly.

Whenever she forgot and told a tale, the tell-tale bird was delighted and at once shouted out a whole lot of things about Tilly!

'Tilly lost her hair-ribbon yesterday! Tilly got smacked this morning for being rude! Tilly had to stay in at school for getting her sums wrong! Tilly broke a cup at tea-time! Tilly's a baby, she spilt her cocoa down her front!'

So the bird went on, and there was no way

of stopping it at all, except by Tilly never telling a tale herself. In about a month Tilly had stopped telling tales. She always thought twice before she spoke now, and became a much nicer little girl. The other children began to like her. She was asked out to tea and made a lot of friends.

And one day the tell-tale bird flew away! It squawked for the last time on the mantelpiece.

'You're no good at telling tales now, Tilly! I'm going to look for someone else! It's no fun here now!' And it spread its blue-and-yellow wings, flew out of the window and disappeared.

I'm not quite sure where it went to – but if you hear people say, 'Ah, a little bird told me!' you may be sure that tell-tale bird is somewhere about, telling tales and secrets just as it did when it was with Tilly!

HE FORGOT HIS EARS

Once upon a time there was a little boy called Pip. His real name was Philip but they called him Pip for short.

He was a good boy and a jolly boy – but oh, how he DID hate washing! It was a most peculiar thing but no sooner had he washed his hands than they seemed dirty again – and as for his face, it always seemed to have a smudge on it. Poor Pip!

But what he got into most trouble about was washing behind his ears. Every single day his mother scolded him because he forgot.

'Pip, you haven't washed *behind* your ears,' she would say. 'Go back to the bathroom at once and wash all round and behind them. Good gracious, there is enough dirt there to grow potatoes!'

So back to the bathroom Pip would have to go and would rub and scrub behind his ears till he was quite clean.

But every morning he forgot again, and in the end his mother got very cross.

'I do wish I hadn't got to tell you *every* morning, Pip!' she said. 'Why can't you remember without being told? You wash in front of your ears – why can't you wash behind too?'

One day Pip's mother went away to stay with Pip's Granny, and Pip was left at home with Ellen the maid. Now Ellen was too busy to bother about how Pip washed himself. So long as his hands were clean she didn't look behind his ears. So you can guess that Pip didn't wash them at all. And my goodness me, they soon needed it!

Pip went to school each day with other boys and girls. And do you know, after his mother had been away a week, a most extraordinary thing happened!

Pip was sitting at the front of the class, and everyone was doing handwork. The children were allowed to talk to one another then, and they loved that lesson. Suddenly the little girl behind Pip began to stare and stare and stare at him. Pip felt her staring and turned round.

'Why are you staring at me?' he said.

'Well, what have you got behind your ears?' asked Mary, the little girl, trying to see.

'Nothing, silly, except hair,' said Pip.

'I can see something green there,' said Mary. 'You feel and see.'

Pip felt – and what a shock he got! There certainly *was* something growing behind his ears – and it wasn't hair! It felt like stalks!

Mary told the boy next to her, and he stared at Pip too. 'It looks as if you've got a plant growing behind your ears,' said George. 'Did you put it behind there for fun?'

Pip didn't answer. He simply couldn't *imagine* what it was. Just then the bell rang and it was the end of school. The children put away their handwork and went to get their hats. Pip got his first and ran off before the others were ready.

He rushed home. He went to the bathroom and looked in the looking-glass there. And do you know what had happened?

Potatoes were growing behind his ears!

'It's just what Mother said would happen!' groaned poor Pip. 'I've been forgetting to wash behind my ears all this week – and I suppose there was enough dirt to grow potatoes! Oh dear, whatever am I to do?'

Really, he did look funny! A potato plant was growing neatly behind each of his ears, sending up nice green stalks with leaves just ready to unfold.

'In a day or two the leaves will open and there will be flowers next!' said Pip. 'How everyone will laugh at me! I wonder if I can pull up the plants – will it hurt me?'

He tried – and it did hurt him! But he managed to get the roots up at last. Then he pulled the other potato plant from behind his second ear. He threw them into the waste-paper basket.

'Now I'll wash my ears well,' he thought. 'I simply WON'T have potatoes growing there. Whatever would Mother say if she saw them!

My goodness, it's a good thing Mary saw them this morning. I mightn't have noticed till they were ever so big, and then how everyone would have laughed at me!'

He washed his ears so well that they looked as red as tomatoes. Pip was sure they had never been so clean before.

When he went to school that afternoon he found Mary and George waiting for him, with everyone else looking excited.

'We told all the children that you were growing potatoes behind your ears,' said George, 'and they want to see them. And we want to know if you have to water them, and what you do to get the potatoes when they are ready.'

'I haven't *got* any potatoes,' said Pip, going red. The children went round him and peeped behind his ears.

'Oh, he hasn't any potatoes growing!' they cried in disappointment. 'Oh, we did so want to see them!'

The school bell rang. Everyone went in. Pip felt the boys and girls were keeping a watch on him to see if potatoes began to grow suddenly again. He did feel uncomfortable. He kept feeling to see if anything was growing – but it wasn't!

Do you know, Pip washed behind his ears at least six times a day until his mother came home. She *was* surprised to see him looking so clean!

'Whatever has changed you, Pip?' she cried.

'Oh, Mother, I grew potatoes behind my ears one day, just as you said I would,' said Pip. 'It was dreadful!'

But I really don't think his mother believed him. Do be careful of *your* ears, won't you!

HE DIDN'T THINK

'Mother, I do think you might let me go and do your shopping sometimes,' said Peter. 'I do really. It would be fun. All the other children do shopping in the town sometimes!'

'I *would* let you, Peter, if only you could be trusted to look where you are going, when you cross the roads,' said his mother. 'But you never think of looking left and right. You don't even stop when you get to the kerb! I am always afraid you will be knocked down.'

'Well, let me take Jock with me,' said Peter. Jock was his dog. Peter loved him with all his heart, and thought he was the best dog in the world. 'You always say I'm safe with him!'

'I certainly think Jock is a very sensible dog!' said Peter's mother. 'He's not a bit silly in traffic as most dogs are. *He* stops at the kerb and looks, first right then left, before he crosses. I only wish you were as sensible!'

'I will, Mother, really, I will!' said Peter. 'Just try me!'

'Well – I suppose you'll have to be trusted sooner or later!' said Mother. 'You can go down to the town tomorrow for the groceries. You can take the big basket with you.'

'Jock can carry it to the shops, when it's empty, and I will carry it back when it's full!' said Peter. He felt rather happy and important. After all, he was seven now. He ought to be allowed to go on errands!

So the next day he took the big basket out of the cupboard and whistled for Jock. The big dog came bounding up. Peter gave him the basket. Jock took the handle in his mouth. Then the two of them set off.

'Now be careful, Peter!' called his mother.

'Of course, Mother!' said Peter. Down the hill he went, and into the town. He came to the first crossing and had to stop because two or three people were there, waiting to cross too. Peter crossed with them. Jock crossed too, still carrying the basket. Everyone smiled to see him. He looked down his nose at the other dogs. Not one of them carried a shopping basket. Jock felt as important as Peter did.

'Hey, Peter! Where are you going?' called Anna from the other side of the road.

'Shopping,' said Peter. 'Can't stop to play this morning, Anna. Goodbye!'

'Peter! Look out for Bobby. He's got a new tricycle!' cried Anna. 'It's a fine one. He might give you a ride.'

So Peter looked out for Bobby, and soon he saw him. He was on the opposite side of the road, and he was on his new tricycle. It was a fine one, painted blue and silver.

'Peter! Come and see my new tricycle!' cried Bobby. And, without thinking at all, Peter at once stepped straight off the kerb and into the road!

He didn't look to the right. He didn't look to the left. He only looked at that fine new tricycle.

Jock saw his little master stepping into the road and he ran to the kerb too. But Jock knew that he must stop and look before he crossed the road. Peter's father had taught him that when he was a puppy! So Jock stood for a moment, basket in mouth, and looked quickly up the road.

A lorry was coming, a big one, loaded with a great stack of wood! Jock knew there would not be time to cross over – but Peter was already in the road! Peter would be knocked down. There was no time for him to cross, and he did not even see the lorry! Jock dropped the basket and gave a loud bark.

Peter took no notice, and Jock knew there was only one thing to do. He must spring into the road, almost under the coming lorry, and knock Peter out of danger. So the big dog leaped off the kerb, sprang onto the little boy, and sent him spinning to the other side, where he fell with a bump. The lorry missed him by an inch, and the lorry-driver tried his best to swerve away from the dog.

But poor Jock could not get out of the way

The big dog leapt off the kerb

in time. One of the wheels ran over his back leg. The dog gave a yelp of pain, and lay still in the road, unable to get up. Peter got up and saw what had happened.

In a trice there was a crowd round. 'The brave dog!' said somebody. 'He pushed the boy out of danger. Silly child – he ran straight out and never even looked to see if anything was coming. But the dog looked.'

Peter was by Jock, crying as if his heart would break. 'Jock! Oh Jock! Are you hurt? Oh, your poor, poor leg! Oh Jock, you saved me, but you got hurt yourself! Why didn't I look as Mother told me to!'

Jock was taken to the animal doctor, and his poor broken leg was set and put into a splint. Peter had to carry him home, crying tears down his cheeks all the way. Jock licked them up as they fell onto his nose. He whined a little.

'Don't be so upset, little master!' he tried to say. 'You're only a little boy who hasn't learnt to think properly yet. I'm a big dog, and I know I must look after you.'

Peter understood, but it didn't make him feel any better. 'I wouldn't be so unhappy if I had hurt myself through my own silliness,' he said. 'But because I didn't think, *you* are hurt, Jock. And maybe you will never be able to run again!'

Well, Jock *can* run, but he runs with a limp. And whenever Peter sees the limp he is sad. You may be sure he thinks now when he crosses the road – but wasn't it a pity that poor Jock had to be hurt, before Peter learnt to be sensible!

THE BOY WHO PUT OUT HIS TONGUE

William was quite a nice boy, but he had one very silly habit. He *would* put out his tongue at people when he was cross or disagreeable!

Now this, as you know, is a rude thing to do, and people didn't like it.

'It spoils William when he sticks out his tongue at me,' said Auntie Hilda.

'I'd give that boy of yours a smacking if he were mine, putting out his tongue at me like that!' roared Uncle Harry.

'Doesn't William look ugly and horrid when he puts out his tongue at us?' said all the school children to one another.

His mother was very upset about it, especially when William actually put out his tongue at *her*. She could hardly believe that her own boy would be so bad-mannered and rude.

That afternoon she went to see William's old nurse, who lived in a cottage at the other end of the village. The old nurse had been William's mother's nurse too, so she was very old indeed. When William's mother told her about her little boy's habit of putting out his tongue at people and making everyone feel cross, the nurse nodded her head.

'Ah, yes!' she said, 'I know a way of curing that! Just send him to me tomorrow, will you? And don't worry if he doesn't come back for a while. He will be quite safe.'

So the next day William's mother sent him to see his old nurse. He was fond of her, and he gave her a hug when he saw her.

'Keep your coat on, William,' she said. 'I just want you to take a walk into the next village for me, and buy me an ounce of red wool.'

So William started off to go to the next village. But somehow the way seemed rather different from any way he had been before. The people he met seemed rather queer too – they were dressed in bright gay colours, and their ears seemed very long and pointed.

'Almost as if they were fairy folk,' said William to himself. He walked along and came to the village. The houses were small and higgledy-piggledy, and the wool shop was very queer indeed, not a bit like William remembered it. The doorway was so low that he had to bend down to get through it, and the shop was very dark.

'An ounce of red wool, please,' he said to the old lady in the shop.

She measured out an ounce, wrapped it up, and gave it to William. He went out again, but the old lady called after him. 'Come back and shut the door, little boy.'

William went back; but before he shut the door he popped his head into the shop and put his red tongue out at the old lady. Wasn't it rude of him?

The old lady jumped up and ran to him. 'Dear, dear,' she said, taking him by the shoulders, 'so your tongue needs seeing to, does it? Put it out again, little boy. Yes, yes, it is not a nice tongue. You need a dose of medicine.'

Still holding William very firmly, she took him to a cupboard. From it she took a big bottle of yellow medicine and poured out a tablespoonful. Then, before William knew what was happening, the spoon was in his mouth and the horrid, horrid medicine was trickling down his throat.

'Oooh! Ah!' spluttered poor William. 'Don't do that.'

'It will do you good,' said the old lady, patting him on the back. 'I'm glad you showed me your tongue just now. I could see you needed a dose of medicine.'

William ran angrily out of the shop. He would dearly have loved to put out his tongue at the old lady again, but he didn't dare to now. He ran down the street.

As he went round the corner, he bumped into someone. It was a little round man with big pointed ears and a tall hat on his head. The hat went spinning into the gutter.

'Now, now, boy,' said the man angrily. 'Pick

He popped his head in at the door and put out his tongue at the old lady

137

up my hat, and next time you turn a corner, look where you are going.'

William picked up the hat; but as he gave it back he put out his tongue at the angry man. In a trice the man caught hold of him and said, 'Dear, dear! Your tongue looks dreadful. Come along home with me and I'll do something about it.'

It was no good William struggling. He had to go with the man. He turned in at a gate on which was a big brass plate that said 'Dr Makemwell.' So the little round man was a doctor. Oooh!

Dr Makemwell took William upstairs and made him get undressed. He popped him into bed and fetched a large bottle of red medicine. He pulled down the blinds and then he spoke to William.

'I'm so glad you showed me your tongue,' he said. 'I could see that you were not at all well, by looking at your tongue. It is quite yellow. Now you must stay in bed all today with the blinds down. You must not read or play. It would be best if you don't have anything to eat, but, if you feel thirsty, drink a little of that medicine by you.'

The doctor went out of the room, and William heard the door being locked. He sat up in a fright. Was he really ill? Could the doctor and the old woman really tell by his tongue whether he was ill or not? Whatever was he to do? He was hungry already, and he couldn't bear the thought of staying in bed all day with nothing to eat. As for that horrid-looking medicine, he wouldn't drink a single drop of it. Not he.

The door was locked, for William tried it. He sat on the bed and wondered what to do. Why did he put out his tongue in that silly way? It had got him into this stupid trouble!

He wondered if the window was open. He went across to see. Yes, it was! Below the window was a sloping roof. If William got out onto that, he could slide down the roof to the gutter, and then jump to the ground. He dressed quickly, hoping that the doctor wouldn't come back. He crept out of the window onto the roof outside. He slid down it quietly. It was a big jump to the ground, but William managed it. Once on the ground, he shot away down the garden to the gate, and out he went, free again!

'I'm jolly well going back home now!' thought William to himself. 'I don't like this village at all. It's not a bit like it was last time I was here.'

He ran down the street. On the other side of the road were some children, all with pointed ears and merry faces. They waved to William.

Did William wave back? No, he did not. He put out his tongue at them. You might think he would remember not to do that, but, you see, it was such a habit with him.

The children stared in surprise; then they all ran after him and caught him.

'He's ill, he's ill!' they cried. 'Did you see him put out his tongue to show us? Come, little boy, we have some pills to make you better.'

'I'm not ill,' said William. 'I'm quite all right, and I don't want any pills.'

'But your tongue is bright yellow,' cried the children. 'Look!'

They stopped William by a mirror in a shop window and he looked at his tongue. The children were quite right – it was bright yellow.

'It must have been that yellow medicine the old lady in the wool shop gave me,' he said. But the children would not believe that. They took him to their schoolroom, which was not far off, and called to a thin, tall lady who wore spectacles and was writing something on the blackboard.

'Teacher, teacher!' they cried. 'Here is a boy with a yellow tongue. He put it out to show us how bad it was. Give him some of your pills.'

'Dear, dear!' said the teacher, and she went to a cupboard. She took out a box of pills and emptied three into her hand. 'Show me your tongue,' she said to William; and as soon as he put it out she popped the three pills into his mouth, held his nose till he swallowed them, and then beamed at him.

'I hope you didn't taste them much,' she said. 'I know they are very horrid.'

'Ooooh!' said poor William, for the pills were just about the horridest he had ever tasted.

'Oooh! Give me a drink of water, please. I can't bear this horrid taste in my mouth.'

The teacher gave him a drink of water. The children went out to play. William felt that he simply couldn't bear this village any longer – what with horrid medicine, and being locked up in a bedroom and then dreadful pills – really, it was terrible! He slipped out of the door and down the street again.

A man on a bicycle nearly knocked him over. But do you suppose William put out his tongue at him? No, he did not! He wasn't going to have any more pills or medicine.

A butcher-boy passed him, whistling loudly. Did William put out his tongue? No, he certainly didn't. He kept it firmly in his mouth, you may be sure, and ran on down the road.

He ran and he ran; and at last he came back to his own village, and there was the cottage of his old nurse. How glad he was to see it! He ran in and gave the old lady a hug.

'Here's your wool,' he said.

'You've been a long time, William,' said the old lady.

William went red. He wasn't going to tell his old nurse all the things that had happened to him! He knew she would laugh.

But there was such a twinkle in her eyes that William couldn't help feeling she knew something. He said goodbye and went home.

He looked at his tongue in the looking-glass.

It was still bright yellow. How dreadful! He must be careful not to let anyone see it – people seemed to be so silly about tongues.

So Willam kept his tongue to himself, and everyone was surprised to find that he no longer put it out when he felt cross or cheeky.

It isn't yellow now – it gradually got right again. That was lucky for William, wasn't it?

All these books are available at your local bookshop or newsagent, or can be ordered from the publisher. To order direct from the publishers just tick the title you want and fill in the form below:

Name _____

Address _____

_____

Send to: Collins Childrens Cash Sales
         PO Box 11
         Falmouth
         Cornwall
         TR10 9EN

Please enclose a cheque or postal order or debit my Visa/ Access –

Credit card no:

Expiry date:

Signature:

– to the value of the cover price plus:

UK: 60p for the first book, 25p for the second book, plus 15p per copy for each additional book ordered to a maximum charge of £1.90.

BFPO: 60p for the first book, 25p for the second book plus 15p per copy for the next 7 books, thereafter 9p per book.

Overseas and Eire: £1.25 for the first book, 75p for the second book. Thereafter 28p per book.

Armada reserve the right to show new retail prices on covers which may differ from those previously advertised in the text or elswhere.

ARMADA

Other titles by
Enid Blyton
in Armada

ARMADA